"Hello, Trace."

A figure stood at the open door to the barn, silhouetted against the white sunlight.

He would know those long legs anywhere. The effect on him was always the same. It began with a constriction in his throat and moved slowly downward to flood his loins with heat.

It was just his cursed luck, feeling this way about another Anglo woman. Accepting the powerful effect she had on him with a mixture of anger and resignation, he came forward. "Hello, Jenna."

He looked so primal and beautiful that it literally stole Jenna's breath away. He was in his element here among the mustangs, his body glistening in the sunshine, his ebony eyes gleaming at her through the shadows.

But in those eyes she saw the age-old hostility of the Sioux staring back at her, and in spite of the pleasant greeting, there was nothing friendly about him.

Dear Reader,

Merry Christmas! I hope you'll like Intimate Moments' gift to you: six wonderful books, perfect for reading by the lights of the Christmas tree. First up is our Heartbreakers title. Welcome veteran romance writer Sara Orwig to the line with *Hide in Plain Sight*. Hero Jake Delancy is tough—but the power of single mom Rebecca Bolen's love is even stronger!

Terese Ramin is back with *Five Kids, One Christmas*, a book that will put you right in the holiday mood. Then try Suzanne Brockmann's *A Man To Die For*, a suspenseful reply to the question "What would you do for love?" Next up is *Together Again*, the latest in Laura Parker's Rogues' Gallery miniseries. *The Mom Who Came To Stay* brings Nancy Morse back to the line after a too-long absence. This book's title says it all. Finally, welcome Becky Barker to the line as she tells the story of *The Last Real Cowboy*.

Six books, six tales of love to make your holidays bright. Enjoy!

Leslie Wainger
Senior Editor and Editorial Coordinator

Please address questions and book requests to:
Silhouette Reader Service
U.S.: 3010 Walden Ave., P.O. Box 1325, Buffalo, NY 14269
Canadian: P.O. Box 609, Fort Erie, Ont. L2A 5X3

THE MOM WHO CAME TO STAY

NANCY MORSE

Published by Silhouette Books

America's Publisher of Contemporary Romance

 SILHOUETTE BOOKS

ISBN 0-373-07683-5

THE MOM WHO CAME TO STAY

Copyright © 1995 by Nancy Morse

This edition published by arrangement with Harlequin Books S.A.

® and TM are trademarks of Harlequin Books S.A., used under
license. Trademarks indicated with ® are registered in the United States
Patent and Trademark Office, the Canadian Trade Marks Office and in
other countries.

Printed in U.S.A.

Books by Nancy Morse

Silhouette Intimate Moments

Sacred Places #181
Run Wild, Run Free #210
The Mom Who Came To Stay #683

NANCY MORSE

Born and raised in New York City, Nancy has lived for the last three years in Florida with her husband of twenty-eight years, Talley, and their Alaskan malamute, Max. An early love of reading and happy endings led to the publication of her first historical romance in 1980. She has an avid interest in Native American history and culture, and takes great pride in her collection of nineteenth-century artifacts. In addition to writing, Nancy enjoys gardening, watching good films, reading and regular aerobic workouts to sweat out the daily frustrations of life.

Chapter 1

Trace McCall went flying through the air and landed flat on his butt on the ground of the dusty corral. Muttering an epithet, he got to his feet and slapped the dust from his jeans. Chest heaving, fists balled in fury, he stood there, watching the buckskin pace the far end of the corral at a nervous gait.

Without warning, the past loomed, as real and as vivid as the moment. It often happened like that, unexpectedly, too many times to count since that cold day in December five years ago. It didn't matter that that was then and this was now, or that he had learned a valuable lesson. The pain of betrayal was always the same. He could shut that window tight, but like the cold Nebraska wind, those memories still kept blowing in.

"He doesn't seem to want you on him."

The sound of a feminine voice, smooth and beguiling, spun Trace's head around. The unexpected
appearance of a woman at the corral rendered him
momentarily speechless. His dark eyes, however, were
in motion, moving over her in a rapid but thorough
appraisal.

She was tall and slender, a good five-seven in her
bare feet, he judged. She was wearing a linen dress in
a natural color that blended with the hue of her skin.
The flared skirt whipped about her calves in the
breeze, pressing provocatively against legs that looked
long and slender. The cap sleeves and the lace-up
front, with its low, scooped neckline, left her smooth
flesh vulnerable to Trace's inspection. Backlit by a
setting sun that ignited small fires through her shoul-
der-length chestnut hair, she was a breathtaking sight,
something Trace would hardly have expected to see
out here in the middle of nowhere. Something tightened instinctively inside him.

"What he doesn't want is of no concern to me," he
said.

Green eyes that reminded Trace of the hills in
springtime stared back at him without wavering. "I
can see that. I just wonder if you made your point."

Trace glanced back to where the buckskin stallion
was moving at a brisk gait. His dark eyes narrowed,
the tiny lines etched into the sun-browned skin around
them hardening with rancor. He was an ugly little
mustang, lean and rangy, the color of untanned cowhide. Trace had herded him in with the others during
spring roundup. He trained the even-tempered ones
for range and trail work and the amiable ones for

pleasure riding, and sold the spirited ones as bucking horses to rodeos around the country. Trace didn't think about breaking a horse; he just did it. Sure, that miserable mustang was more ornery than most, but that didn't mean he couldn't be broken and turned into an acceptable mount.

He turned back to her and said, "I think I've made the point that I'm not about to give up."

From where she had watched at the gate to the corral, Jenna had already gotten that impression. She hadn't failed to notice, either, the graceful way he moved, in spite of the eddies of dust kicked up by furious hooves. It had called to mind the image of an antelope she'd seen bounding through the breaks in long, graceful strides that had literally taken her breath away. She had experienced the same constriction in her lungs watching Trace McCall in action.

There was no denying the dangerous thrill she derived from observing the primal game being enacted in the corral, yet Jenna hadn't driven to this remote corner of the Santee Sioux Indian Reservation just to watch Trace McCall break a mean-tempered mustang.

Watching the horse with a mixture of grimness and admiration, Jenna remarked, "All that pride. Why would anyone want to break it?"

His wolflike eyes studied her profile, caught against the diffused light of sunset. Again that tightening, like a fist deep inside of him.

"He might as well learn that pride only gets in the way."

There was no mistaking the bitterness lurking in the deep tone of his voice. Jenna turned to look at him. "I would have thought that if anything is in *your* way, Mr. McCall, it's pride. Why else would you be so hell-bent on breaking that horse? Why not just let him go?"

Why else? There were a hundred reasons he could have given her. A thousand. Or just one. He was an Indian. That was the reason for everything. The cause of everything. But he wasn't about to explain that to her.

"That horse represents income to me. I didn't bring in as many mustangs this year. I can't afford to let him go. And say, who are you, anyway?"

"I'm Jenna Ward."

When that produced no visible sign of recognition in his dark eyes, she prompted, "KayCee's teacher at the Yankton Elementary School. Didn't KayCee tell you I was coming? You *did* get the note I sent home with her, didn't you?"

He vaguely recalled KayCee going on one morning at breakfast about a new teacher at school, but he'd only been half listening. Jenna Ward sure didn't look like any schoolteacher he'd ever seen. He wondered if there was some young schoolboy wearing his heart on his sleeve for the pretty teacher. A boyfriend, maybe? A husband? Trace didn't like the route his thoughts were taking, and he shifted into another gear.

"Note? Sure. Sure, I got it." He remembered now the note that was still folded on the kitchen counter, waiting to be read. Damn, he'd meant to get around to reading it.

"Then why do I get the distinct impression that you didn't expect to see me today?" Or any other day, for that matter, judging from the look on his face, Jenna thought sourly.

"I thought you'd be earlier, that's all," he replied, trying to mask the fact that he'd had no idea she was coming, or why she was here.

"I meant to come earlier," she confessed. "I got a late start after all the papers I graded this morning, and the stops I made along the way."

Deftly Trace coiled the lariat in his hand. "So, what's on your mind, Miss Ward?"

He was brutally to the point, but that was all right. She hadn't come here to beat around the bush.

"It's KayCee, Mr. McCall."

"What's she done now?"

"It's not what she's done. It's what she *doesn't* do."

Trace rolled his eyes. "And they say we Indians are hard to understand. All right, what *doesn't* KayCee do?"

"Her homework. Her schoolwork. She's falling behind, and I'm concerned. You should be, too."

Defensively he responded, "I sent her to summer school, didn't I?"

Jenna chose her next words carefully, for something told her that this man could be as hard to approach as that mustang he was trying to break.

"It's not summer school. It's not what she's learning or what she's not learning in school. In fact, I don't think it's school at all. I think it's something more.''

"If you have something to say, say it."

Jenna was finding out the hard way that Trace McCall was not an easy man to like. There was a chip the size of a redwood on his shoulder that she would have loved to knock off. Yet, in spite of the inner voice that cautioned her not to press him, she answered candidly.

"It's something she's lacking. KayCee is a very unhappy little girl. What I keep asking myself is, why?"

His uneasy shifting from one foot to the other spoke volumes. Here it comes, he thought grimly. She was about to tell him what a rotten father he was. And the truth of it was, she was probably right. He knew he worked too hard, but hell, someone had to pay the bills. And besides, he couldn't be up on a bucking horse and brooding over the past at the same time. Throwing himself into his work helped take his mind off the loneliness of the present and soothe the pain of rejection that smarted even now, five years later. He knew KayCee was unhappy, but short of rewriting history, what could he do? He didn't need to hear these things from Jenna Ward, but neither could he have blamed her for saying them.

"You know how it is," he said. "The kid comes from a broken home. These days, who doesn't?"

"Mr. McCall, I really don't think—"

"I come from a broken home myself," he said, overriding her objection. "She's a good kid, though. You watch, she'll shape up."

Jenna stared back at him with disbelief. "That's it? She'll shape up? That's all you have to say?"

"I know my daughter. I'm telling you, KayCee'll be all right."

"And I'm telling you that she won't be. Not all by herself. A twelve-year-old needs help, Mr. McCall. And I'm beginning to think she doesn't get much of that here at home."

Jenna thought she'd gone too far when he made a slight movement toward her. Through the fabric of his shirt, she could see his muscles tense. She had touched a sensitive nerve in the hard-edged man.

Angrily Trace demanded, "Are you licensed to make judgments like that?"

"I call it the way I see it."

"And just what have you seen? How would you know what goes on here at home?"

"I see what KayCee brings to the classroom," Jenna argued. "And I'm not talking about a brown paper bag with her lunch in it. Although, while I'm on that subject, I might suggest a slight divergence from peanut-butter-and-jelly sandwiches and candy bars. Tell me, Mr. McCall, have you ever heard of fruit?"

"KayCee doesn't like fruit."

"Really? That's odd. I could have sworn I saw her steal an apple from another child's lunch box the other day."

"It's only an apple," he said. "Hardly a felony."

Jenna did her best to ignore the pointed sarcasm. "You should see her. During recess, she sits by herself, and doesn't participate in any of the games the other children play."

"KayCee's always been a serious little girl," Trace offered.

"Serious is one thing. Sad is another."

What did she know about it? How could she possibly understand the Indian way? He was silent for a long moment as he battled with himself over whether or not to explain.

In a low and grudging voice, he said, "We Indians teach our children to take care of themselves, to do things by themselves. Once it was necessary for survival to learn ways of self-reliance. Here on the reservations, it still is. I was taught in the old way, and that's how I'm raising my daughter." What he didn't say was that he didn't need an intruder coming here and telling him how to do it.

"Does the old way call for parents to stand by idle when their children need help?" Jenna questioned.

"I don't restrict KayCee. If she stumbles, she's got to learn how to get up. If she needs help, I'll help her, but I'm not about to stand over her with psychological tests or punish her every time she disobeys Dr. Spock. Some people say our way is too permissive, but a kid grows up to be strong and independent."

Calling to mind the stubborn independence she'd witnessed in the classroom, Jenna realized that KayCee McCall had inherited more than her dark Indian looks from her father. She could only guess at how much of his pigheadedness ran through the child's veins, as well.

"I'll admit that in the time I've been teaching at the elementary school, I haven't gotten to know KayCee very well," said Jenna. "She seems to resist all attempts to draw her closer. It doesn't take a genius, however, to see that she's unhappy."

Trace seized upon her truthfulness. "If you admit to not knowing her very well, how do you know she's unhappy?"

Jenna had watched enough of the furious scene in the corral to know that this wouldn't be easy for her. "For your information, Mr. McCall, I, too, come from a broken home. My parents divorced when I was three, and I spent my formative years being shuttled back and forth between them. I may not be an Indian, but like KayCee, I'm a female. And I, too, was once twelve years old. I'd say that makes me more in tune to what your daughter is feeling than you are. And from what I've seen here today, I wouldn't be surprised if that was part of the problem."

"Do you always do that?"

"Do what?"

"Analyze. You seem to do an awful lot of it."

"Perhaps I should explain."

His eyes never left her face as he replied sardonically, "That would be nice."

Jenna had dealt with difficult parents before, but she'd never encountered anything like this. Not only was Trace McCall a stubborn man, and proud beyond belief, but she sensed something simmering deep inside of him. A memory, a hurt—whatever it was, it had left its bitter traces in his eyes. She suspected that he wasn't very different from that horse he was trying to break—strong and proud, mean-tempered sometimes, the kind that didn't run with the herd. And lonely. She could see that also in his eyes.

Dealing with him was even more difficult than she'd imagined it would be, because, much as she hated to admit it, she found herself attracted to him. It was a raw, basic kind of attraction that she told herself was purely physical, the way any woman would react to a virile man. Even now she could feel the warmth rising to the surface of her skin as he scrutinized her.

The truth was, Jenna had never seen anything like him. He had the coal-dark eyes of an Indian. His hair was jet black and shiny, falling without so much as a ripple to his shoulders. Several long, straight strands spilled over the top of the bandanna that was knotted around his forehead, slicing his high, angular cheek in the wind. His face was darkly bronzed, with lean, hawkish features. He was not handsome by any standard Jenna had ever known, yet there was something magnificent about those hard, lean angles, and she suspected that he might be brutally handsome, if only he would smile.

He was broad-shouldered and strong-muscled, no doubt from the rigorous work he did on the ranch. A long, sinewy body was encased in dusty jeans that were torn at the knees, a blue chambray shirt with sleeves that spanned well-defined biceps and buttons that were opened to reveal a smooth-skinned chest, a vest of tanned cowhide, and well-worn lizard-skin cowboy boots with scuffed heels. She noticed that he hadn't bothered to remove his leather riding gloves.

It was a clear sign that he wasn't about to shake hands with her or make her feel welcome.

Somewhere deep inside her, Jenna sensed that he would be a hard man to love, the kind who left a woman's heart as bruised as her lips. For one crazy moment, she found herself wondering if his love-making would match the reckless and harsh passion she saw in his eyes. A covey of wings flapped madly in the pit of her stomach when she dared to imagine what his kiss would be like. Harsh and punishing, no doubt, judging from the hostility she saw in his eyes, but wildly sensual, as well, judging from the rest of him.

Jenna's whole system seemed to go wild for a moment, sending off signals that she prayed were not mirrored on her face. She cleared her throat and said, "You see, I majored in psychology, thinking that one day I would open my own practice. I began teaching to pay the bills, and felt I could really make a difference, so I've been doing it ever since."

"I find it hard to believe that you're teaching at the Yankton Elementary School because you couldn't find a job somewhere else."

Jenna could feel the heat seeping into her cheeks, caused in part by her body's reaction to him, in part by his provoking manner. "You're wrong if you think that, Mr. McCall. I'm here because I care about kids. I really do. Five years of teaching school on the Lower East Side of Manhattan should attest to that. Avenues A, B and C—Alphabet City, they call it—where I've seen things that would make your skin crawl. I know an unhappy child when I see one."

"But I'm her father," Trace protested. "Don't you think I'd know if my own daughter was in trouble?"

"Not necessarily. Parents are sometimes the last ones to see it." She aimed a sidelong look up at him and said slyly, "You could consider that I'm doing you a favor."

He heaved a disgruntled sigh and muttered, "I'm afraid to ask."

"I'll lay it on the line to you. Either you speak to me about this, or you can speak to someone at the Department of Social Services."

"This is an Indian reservation, Miss Ward. Haven't you ever heard of sovereignty? Your Department of Social Services has no jurisdiction here."

"The Bureau of Indian Affairs, then."

A short, bitter laugh broke from his throat. "Yeah, right." He was clearly unimpressed.

"The head of the tribal council, then."

"What makes you think they'll listen to what you have to say?"

"What makes you think they won't?" she countered.

This time Trace didn't have an offhand remark to toss back at her. Although the tribal council lacked any real political power, he knew that they took matters relating to the family very seriously. So, the pretty schoolteacher had done her homework.

"All right," he said, relenting. "Let me take care of Mr. Charm over there. Then we'll talk." He turned and walked away with long, lithe strides that had Jenna's eyes glued to the dusty seat of his pants.

He unfurled the lariat as he approached the buckskin. The rope circled over his head, hovering on the dry Nebraska wind before sailing through the air and landing around the horse's neck.

He led the buckskin to a small corral behind the barn. When he returned to where he'd left Jenna, she was gone. His eyes scanned the area with unexpected eagerness and spotted her standing on the perimeter of a grove of pine trees about fifty yards away.

The cool air beckoned to her from beneath the pines. It was dark there, except for a random ray of fading sunlight that slanted through the thick branches. Jenna felt the perspiration evaporate from her overheated flesh the moment she stepped in amid the trees. It had been a long day, and she was tired, but beneath the leafy canopy, away from the cold scrutiny of those dark eyes that seemed to look right through her, she felt her muscles begin to unwind.

She never heard him come up behind her. Like the wind, he was suddenly just there. Into her nostrils wafted the aroma of leather, mingled with the scent of a hardworking man. Her muscles tightened up again. The sound of his voice, low, softly stirring, from deep in his chest, snapped the tension that was strung like a live wire in the air.

"I come here sometimes at night after KayCee's asleep. It's peaceful here. It helps me get my thoughts straight."

Struck by candor she hadn't expected, Jenna turned and looked at him through the growing darkness, eyes searching for an explanation of the quiet desperation she thought she'd heard in his voice.

There was none. All she saw was the unfriendly expression she was more accustomed to.

Did she know what she was doing, Trace wondered, coming to this place that was private to him? This dark and quiet place where there was no escape from his thoughts.

"I presume you took the ferry over."

Jenna nodded. The Yankton Indian Reservation, where she taught at the tribal elementary school, was on the opposite side of the Missouri. A crudely built but effective ferry had transported her and her car across the river to the Santee reservation. From there it had been a twenty-mile-drive to the small ranch where KayCee McCall lived with her father.

"How do you plan on getting back?" he inquired.

"The same way I got here."

"I hate to have to tell you this, but the ferry broke down earlier today. It must've happened just after you got here." He had wondered why he got that phone call earlier, telling him about the breakdown. He realized now that she must have mentioned to the ferry operator that she was on her way to see him. "It happens from time to time. The thing's old. It's a wonder it's lasted this long."

Jenna bit the corner of her lip as she assessed her options. "I can check into a motel."

"You could, if there was one. Or you could stay here tonight."

Trace couldn't believe he'd just said that. Was he crazy? The last thing he needed was some white woman hanging around, telling him how to raise his daughter, churning things up inside of him that he would rather forget. He already knew how dangerous white women could be. He wasn't about to make the same mistake again.

"That's very kind of you, Mr. McCall, but I wouldn't want to inconvenience you."

Trace breathed an inward sigh of relief, and yet, to his own chagrin, he heard himself say, "It's no inconvenience at all. You can use the spare room."

Jenna hesitated. This was not what she had planned.

"Tomorrow's Sunday," said Trace. "No school."

"It's not that. It's just—" How could she tell him that the source of her reluctance was him? She was uncomfortable enough just being in his presence. She wasn't at all sure she wanted to be in his home. And yet she was intrigued by him. She didn't know how it was possible for a man to warn her to stay away with his unfriendly demeanor and yet seem to beg her to come closer with that look in his eyes, but that was the conflicting message she was getting. Hostility and vulnerability, a dangerous combination under any circumstance.

"I—I have work to do," she stammered. "Papers to grade."

She expected—even hoped, in a crazy way—that he would try to coerce her into staying. But the dogged determination she had witnessed in the hot and dusty corral was absent beneath the sweet-smelling pines. She was unprepared for the negligent lifting of his shoulders, as if to suggest that it made no difference to him what she did, or for the way he simply turned and walked away.

"Suit yourself," he said. "KayCee'll probably be disappointed."

The well-placed reminder of KayCee made Jenna feel selfish for thinking only of herself. After all, it was for KayCee's benefit that she'd come out here today. Wasn't helping the girl more important than her own misgivings?

She ran to catch up with Trace. "On second thought, I think I'll take you up on your offer to stay the night."

She didn't see the smile that spread slowly across his lips, or hear the slightly missed heartbeat deep inside his chest.

At the house, the wooden steps to the porch creaked beneath their feet, and the weathered planks vibrated from the thud of Trace's bootheels. He reached for the screen door and paused to look back at her.

A ray of moonlight struck his face at an odd angle. Jenna caught her breath. When had the sun gone down? When had he turned so devastatingly handsome? She blinked her eyes. The way he stood there, looking hard at her, she could almost imagine that his shirt was made of buckskin instead of cotton, that the faded bandanna knotted at the back of his head was a beaded headband laced with feathers, that it was a war lance in his grip, instead of the frame of a screen door. In another time he would have been a warrior, legs naked instead of wrapped in blue denim, spread wide around the girth of a painted war-pony, instead of that rangy buckskin mustang, making war on the whites, just as Jenna sensed he was doing right now with her.

Her voice drifted softly and without forethought into the still night air. "I'm not your enemy."

Inwardly Trace was aghast. How could she know what he was thinking? She was beautiful, she was white, and he wanted her. She was his enemy, all right.

The rusted hinges squeaked when he pushed the screen door open and walked inside.

Chapter 2

KayCee McCall sat at the kitchen table, staring morosely down at the beef stew on her plate, picking at the boiled red potatoes and onions with the tip of her fork.

She had dreaded bringing that note home from school, and now Miss Ward was here, no doubt to talk to her father about that stupid apple she'd stolen from Billy Hobbs's lunch box. She'd only taken it to give to the buckskin. Her dad would skin her alive if he knew she'd been sneaking out at night to feed him.

KayCee looked up from her thoughts when the screen door opened and her father walked in, followed by Jenna Ward. His dark mood was reflected in his eyes.

"KayCee, why don't you get Miss Ward something to eat?"

Her father was tired; she could hear it in his voice. Knowing not to argue, she rose silently.

Jenna spoke up. "Oh, no, please don't. I don't want to impose."

Trace strode to the sink, where he removed his riding gloves and slapped them down on the Formica countertop. "You must be hungry," he said as he rinsed his hands under running water. "I know I am."

He dried his hands on a dish towel and tossed it on the counter. "You can wash up if you want. The bathroom's through there."

Jenna followed his nod out of the kitchen and through the living room to the bathroom, where she washed the dry Nebraska dust from her face and hands, ran her fingers through her hair and smoothed the wrinkles from her dress.

On her way back to the kitchen, she paused to look around. Most of the homes Jenna visited on the Yankton and Santee reservations were small, apartment-size dwellings that were part of subsidized housing developments, or crude shacks out in the rural areas. Stylish furnishings were rare, thanks to the high unemployment rate among reservation Indians. Items such as televisions and refrigerators were luxuries that could be afforded in only a few homes.

The McCall house, on the other hand, while far from lavish, was neat and comfortable. Chintz curtains on the windows matched the roll-arm sofa. Pretty floral prints matted in pastels were framed on the walls. The patina of the old oak furnishings and the scent of linseed oil gave the place a homey feel.

Her attention was drawn to a framed sepia-toned photograph of an elderly Indian woman on the table beside the couch.

"That was my grandmother. The photographer had a hell of a time getting that shot. Some of the old-timers still believe that if you take their picture, you're stealing their souls."

Jenna turned at the deep voice that spoke from behind her. Trace stood in the doorway, his six-foot frame seeming to take up the entire space, one broad shoulder leaning indolently against the jamb. He had removed the bandanna from around his head so that his hair fell unrestricted to his shoulders. Silk, she thought fleetingly, that's what it looked like. Ribbons of thick black silk that screamed to be touched.

She could see the frayed tip of the red bandanna jutting from the side pocket of his jeans. Her eyes followed a natural line down the column of a muscular thigh and back up, to that place by the zipper of his jeans that was faded and worn from the continual press of his male anatomy against the vulnerable denim.

Jenna cleared her throat and forced her attention away from his virility. "You have a lovely home."

He accepted the compliment without a word of gratitude. "We have KayCee's mom to thank for it," he said matter-of-factly. "She was kind enough to take only her suitcase when she left."

That explained the distinct touch of a woman in the decor, and the absence of a Mrs. McCall, but Jenna felt the presence of a bitter memory and let the remark pass without comment.

In the kitchen, KayCee spooned the stew into two bowls, then stood back in acute silence to watch them, and her father in particular. He sure was acting funny tonight. She'd never seen him so nervous. Twice he'd dropped his fork before getting a grasp of it.

Trace was indeed feeling nervous. This was the first time a woman had been in the house since Sylvie, but it was best not to think about that. And KayCee wasn't helping matters any by standing there and staring at them. He turned to his daughter and inquired impatiently, "Don't you have homework to do?"

"I don't give the children homework over the weekend," Jenna explained. "They work hard enough during the week." She paused, adding pointedly, "At least some of them do."

Trace stiffened at the reminder. "KayCee, why don't you go on upstairs?"

"Aw, Dad..." the girl whined.

"Go on. Miss Ward and I have things to talk about. I'll be up in a little while."

They watched her move sulking from the room before they settled into an awkward silence. As they ate, Jenna tried to pretend that she wasn't aware of his eyes on her from across the table, but there it was again, that simmering heat that rose to the surface of her cheeks whenever he looked at her. She wished he would say something, *any*thing, but he seemed to have closed up like a clam.

To break the tense silence, she said, "This is delicious. Who's the cook?"

"KayCee."

"I'm impressed. Her mother taught her well."

Trace laughed, but it was a sound without humor. "If KayCee's mom taught her anything, it was how to cut good corners around barrels."

"I beg your pardon?"

"You know, barrel racing. It's one of the events at a rodeo. They set up three barrels to form a triangular course, and the riders gallop around them, doing a 360-degree turn at each barrel before crossing the finish line. The run is timed, and the fastest time wins." He shook his head. "It was from my mother that my daughter learned to cook, so at least she learned something worthwhile."

"You don't consider barrel racing worthwhile?"

"I suppose it is, if that's what you want to do."

"But *you* don't think so?"

Trace responded with a groan. "Don't you ever take a break from doing that?"

She looked at him from across the table. In those dark Indian eyes, she saw visible signs of annoyance. "Doing what?"

"Analyzing."

Jenna smiled sheepishly. "Oh, that. I'm sorry."

His look softened, but his eyes didn't budge from her face. "Forget it."

Jenna fidgeted under his stare. "I want to thank you again for your hospitality, Mr. McCall."

"Do me a favor, would you," said Trace, "and quit calling me Mr. McCall? It makes me uncomfortable. Call me Trace. Everyone else does."

"That's an interesting name. Does it have some kind of significance?"

His laughter startled her. This time it was a reaction to something he found genuinely funny. "I guess you could say that. My father walked out on my mother before I was born. She used to say that I was the only trace left of him."

"That must have been rough for you."

The casual lifting of his shoulders neither confirmed nor denied her observation. "You deal with it as best you can. Besides, I figure if the guy ran out on us, he wasn't worth having around in the first place."

"McCall doesn't sound very Indian," she said.

"That's because it's not. My grandmother was married to a white man named Henry McCall. He ran a trading post on the Yankton reservation."

He rose from the table, pushing his chair away with the backs of his legs. "Excuse me, would you? I want to go up and talk to KayCee. Help yourself to seconds, if you're still hungry. Or anything else you want."

Upstairs, Trace knocked on the door and entered KayCee's bedroom. Tacked to the walls were posters in blooming color of young TV stars, interspersed with stark black-and-white images of Sitting Bull and Geronimo. His daughter was an Indian, Trace thought proudly, but she was also no different from twelve-year-olds anywhere else. He felt a small surge

of triumph. That should prove to the pretty schoolteacher that she was wrong about KayCee.

KayCee was sitting on the bed, watching television. The bed sagged when Trace sat down on the
edge. He picked up the remote control, aimed it at the
TV and pressed the mute button. Turning to his
daughter, he asked, "Is there anything you want to
tell me?"

She looked away guiltily. "You mean about the
apple?"

"The what? Oh, the apple. No, I meant—"

"Okay, so I took it. Big deal. I didn't mean to. It
was just there. And besides, Billy didn't want it."

"How do you know that?"

"Why else didn't he eat it with the rest of his
lunch?"

Trace heaved a sigh of frustration. Why was it that
whenever his daughter did something questionable,
she always found a reason to justify it? She was just
like her mother in that respect. Just like Sylvie.
Hadn't Sylvie been able to justify walking out on
them five years ago? The rodeo, of course. She
wanted to be a star and there was no stopping her.
He'd been devastated in the face of such logic.

"Every day he brings an apple," KayCee was saying. "Sometimes he eats it, sometimes he doesn't."

Caught up in the painful memory, Trace snapped,
"Forget the apple!"

"You mean you're not mad at me for taking it?"

"No. I mean yes, sure I'm mad. I didn't teach you
to steal. But I wasn't talking about that. Is there
something else you want to tell me?"

She looked at him quizzically. Had he found out about her nighttime visits to the corral? "Wh-what do you mean?"

Trace fidgeted on the edge of the bed. Damn, this was hard. "Maybe there's something on your mind. Something you want to talk about."

"Well . . ." she began tentatively.

He braced himself for her reply, for he had a sinking feeling that Jenna Ward was right. He remembered a time when it hadn't been this way. When he and KayCee had done lots of things together. But then Sylvie had walked out, that day in December, and everything had changed.

"There's this boy at school. His name's Danny. I really like him, but he doesn't know I'm alive. I want him to notice me, but I don't know how. My friend Ellen, she liked this boy once, and she stuffed tissues down the front of her blouse to get him to notice her."

"What? Don't you do any such thing. If that boy doesn't like you for who you are and what you have, he's not worth it."

"But, Dad, I saw this magazine over at Ellen's house—I think it was her brother's—and there were these real pretty naked ladies in it, and they all had such big...such big..." The color rushed to her high-boned cheeks. "You know."

He wanted to take her by the shoulders and shake her hard and tell her that if he ever caught her looking at magazines like that, he'd tan her hide but good. But he was too embarrassed to admit that he knew damn well what was inside those magazines.

"Look," he said, trying to sound casual, but feeling the panic rising within, "not every man likes a woman with such big...you know. In fact, some men like women who are built kind of small."

Like Jenna Ward, he thought, whose small, round breasts would fit perfectly in the palms of his hands. He shoved the outrageous thought from his mind and tried to concentrate on his daughter's dilemma.

"Just be yourself, KayCee." He got up and started for the door. "It's getting late, and I've got to go downstairs and talk to Miss Ward."

"Do you like her, Dad?"

"Miss Ward? Sure. Why wouldn't I like her?"

"No, I mean, do you *like* her?"

He knew what she meant, but what could he say? That the pretty schoolteacher stirred up his hormones like a hornet's nest? That just the thought of her sitting downstairs, alone in the kitchen, made his blood boil? That he found himself wanting her with a fierceness he couldn't remember feeling for any woman, even Sylvie? How could he explain lust to a twelve-year-old?

"Go to sleep, KayCee."

"Dad?"

He paused at the door to aim an impatient look back at her.

"There's the rodeo over at Crandall next Sunday. Remember, I told you about it?"

Trace tensed inside. "I remember."

"You said we could go."

"I said I'd think about it."

"But, Dad, Mom's gonna be there."

His dark eyes strayed to the framed photograph on the night table beside the bed. A pretty woman with blond hair and sparkling blue eyes smiled back at him. A muscle twitched at the corner of his mouth, pulling it downward into a frown.

His gaze returned to his daughter's dark, pleading eyes. No one would have guessed from looking at her that the girl was half-white. Trace was grateful that she didn't resemble her mother. Who needed that painful reminder on a daily basis? He ran a hand through his hair, sweeping the long black locks from his eyes. He was tired. His muscles ached from battling with that damned mustang. His blood was boiling, thanks to that woman in his kitchen. And now this.

"Did she tell you that she was going to be there?"

"No, but—"

"We'll talk about it in the morning."

Downstairs, in the kitchen, the aroma of brewing coffee greeted Trace.

"I hope you don't mind," said Jenna. "You said to help myself, and I thought you could use a cup of strong black coffee."

He inhaled deeply and let out a long, low breath through pursed lips. "You got that right."

"Unless you'd prefer something else. I looked in the refrigerator and didn't see any beer."

"Coffee's fine," Trace replied wearily. "I don't drink."

Jenna had witnessed firsthand the toll that alcohol took on the reservations, and knew that liquor was often used to dull the ache of boredom and futility that plagued reservation life. She was relieved to hear that Trace was an exception, but then, there was nothing typical about Trace McCall.

She placed a cup of steaming black coffee before him on the table. Into her own cup, she poured a little milk, and then she took a seat across from him.

"How'd you know I drink it black?" he asked.

Jenna took a sip of coffee and peered at Trace from over the rim of her cup. The man positively exuded strength. How could he drink his coffee any way but black? "A lucky guess," she replied.

His features softened into a smile. "Thanks."

"You're welcome, Trace."

It was the way she spoke his name, simply, naturally and with a touch of huskiness, that made the smile fade from Trace's face, for against his will he found himself liking the sound of it and wanting to hear it again. The moment of amiability passed as his dark eyes retreated from hers with a quickness that spoke of regret.

"Is KayCee all right?" she asked.

"Sure. Why wouldn't she be?" He struggled for self-control. God, she was pretty. That smile of hers could melt the hardest heart. Who knew? Maybe even his own, if he wasn't careful. He caught himself thinking of a dozen ways he would like to make love to this woman. Right here and now, on the kitchen table, was a good place to start.

"It's not every day the teacher pays a call," said Jenna.

"She thinks it's because of the apple."

"In a way, it is."

He shook his head. "I don't get it. KayCee never stole anything before. Why'd she do it?"

"My guess is it was for the attention."

"But she had to know I'd be mad as hell about it."

"Of course. That's the point. If you get angry, you've got to pay attention to her. The apple is just a symptom, Trace. The problem lies much deeper than that. Do you mind if I ask you a question? Do you and KayCee spend much time together?"

The look on his face gave the answer before he spoke in a low, reluctant voice. "Not so much anymore."

"Perhaps you could get her involved in some of the things you do here on the ranch. She's capable of much more than cooking dinner."

"There's enough for her to do here, what with her chores and all."

"How about something just for fun, then, like a movie?"

He gave her a skeptical look. "Have you seen any movie theaters around lately?"

"Okay, how about a picnic?"

He rolled his eyes at the prospect, but Jenna was undaunted. At least he was no longer claiming that there wasn't a problem. That was a start.

"I heard the kids at school yesterday talking about a rodeo in Crandall next Sunday. Why don't you take KayCee?"

Inwardly Trace winced. "No, no, I don't think so. I...I have a lot of work to do on the ranch. And there's that mustang to break and...and... No, Sunday's not a good day for me." His face was flushed, and he looked uncharacteristically flustered. In response to the curious way she was looking at him, he began, "It's just that—"

"There's no need to explain," said Jenna. She felt suddenly sorry for him, for she sensed that she had touched a tender chord deep inside him. "So do something else with her. I have a feeling that KayCee would love to spend time with you, no matter what you do."

She felt him retreating behind a wall of stony solitude. Before the door was shut tight, she said softly, "Think about it, Trace. It'll do you both some good."

"Yeah. Sure." He got up from the table. "Hey, listen, I'm bushed, and I've got an early day tomorrow. Come on. I'll show you to your room."

Nothing had been settled, and Jenna's mission was far from accomplished, but she didn't press it. She, too, was tired and in no mood to debate the issue with him. Tomorrow she'd get to the heart of this matter.

She followed him upstairs to a small bedroom at the end of the hall, where a twin bed covered in a chenille spread looked comfortable and inviting.

"We keep this room ready for my mother when she comes to visit." He went to the window and drew the curtains aside. "You should get a nice breeze for a while. Then everything gets real still and hot. If it gets too uncomfortable, you can use the fan." He gestured to indicate a small oscillating fan on the oak dresser.

He turned back to her. "Well, good night, then."

"Trace?"

His pulse quickened. "Yes?"

"Is there something I could change into? You know, to sleep in?"

It was so easy to imagine Jenna Ward naked in bed that he hadn't thought of offering her something to wear. "Oh, sure. Hold on. I'll be right back."

He disappeared from the room and returned several minutes later. "Will this do?" In his hand he held one of his T-shirts.

"Yes, thank you, this will be fine."

There was something about him that made the breath stick in her throat and her muscles knot up. It was only when she was alone in bed with the light out that Jenna was finally able to breathe easily. Turning over, she closed her eyes and fell asleep.

It was sometime after midnight. The breeze had died and the air was hot and still, just as Trace had promised it would be. The sound of the creaking hinges of the screen door disturbed the stillness when the tall, shadowed figure left the house and headed for the trees.

Trace often went to the grove when he couldn't sleep. There his thoughts would twist and turn and find their way back to the past. Eventually he would fall asleep, only to awaken when the first faint traces of dawn tinted the horizon, and then he would make his way back to his bed until it was time to get up and start the day.

On this night, he sat for hours with his back pressed up against the trunk of a tree, listening to the crickets under the leaves and the bullfrogs down by the stream, wondering what he was going to do about KayCee.

Lately she'd begun to ask questions, about her body, the things she was feeling inside, questions that only a woman could answer. It was hard raising a daughter without her mother.

His head fell back against the rough bark. Through the dense branches overhead he got a tired glimpse of the sky, dark and studded with stars. He inhaled deeply, drawing the earth-scented air into his lungs, and let it out in a long, low breath as memories of Sylvie loomed up in his weary mind.

She was the daughter of the white man who ran the electronics factory on the old Yankton Sioux reservation across the river. Her father had threatened to disown her when he discovered that she'd been sneaking off to see an Indian. But then she'd gotten pregnant, and marrying an Indian had suddenly been better than having an illegitimate child.

It was the first time Trace had ever had anything of real value in his life. She'd been beautiful and spirited and white—forbidden fruit to an Indian from the wrong side of the river. He'd been a novelty to her, a means of infuriating her father.

He could still see the look on Sylvie's face that August afternoon he'd taken her to observe the sun dance. She had made fun of the ceremonies, which she hadn't understood, and although he himself took no part in the rituals of the sun dance, in a way she had denigrated him, as well. After all, they were his people, his customs, his heritage. It had been the first time he realized that, were it not for the baby they had made together, she would never have married him.

He couldn't help but think of Sylvie and feel again that old sting of regret. He'd always known about her dream of being a star in the rodeo. He'd just never thought she'd give up everything, including him and KayCee, to pursue that dream. And now KayCee wanted to see her mother, the sweetheart of the rodeo, and Trace suddenly found himself immersed in a dilemma.

He didn't know if Sylvie would be performing in the rodeo, but he couldn't take the chance. Why put KayCee through unnecessary pain? The letters that came were few and far between, the phone calls quick, offering little hope that KayCee would see her mother anytime soon. Trace preferred it that way, for lurking deep within him, overshadowed by his proud and arrogant nature, was the fear he kept hidden, that Sylvie would see the pretty little girl KayCee was growing into and want her back. He knew what it was like to grow up without much of anything, how it had felt to lose the woman he thought he loved, how to take what he wanted from a life in which nothing came easy. But for all the survival skills he had learned in his thirty-eight years, he still didn't know how to deal with the prospect of losing KayCee.

After Sylvie left, his mother had told him to stick to his own kind, women who would not scorn him for what he was or walk out on him for what he was not. There had been a few women in his life since then. Full-bloods, mixed-bloods—it didn't make any difference, for none had ever moved him enough for him to stay for more than just a night. Until today, that is, when the green-eyed schoolteacher had walked into his life.

He told himself that he wanted Jenna Ward for purely lustful reasons. What man in his right mind wouldn't be attracted to the slant of those green eyes? Why did she have to look at him the way she had, as if she were as attracted to him as he was to her? He'd be seeing those eyes in his dreams for a long time to come. And what was it about her hair that made him want to crush it in his fingers? And that body, lean and limber, yet round in all the right places.

Lots of women had smooth skin and inviting smiles, but there was something about this woman in particular that sent warning bells off in Trace's mind. It wasn't just the loveliness of those long-lashed eyes; it was the way they looked at him, bold and unafraid. It wasn't merely the sound of her voice, husky and beguiling, that sent ripples of pleasure down his spine at the simple utterance of his name; it was the things she said, the outspoken nerve of the woman, which had a surprisingly thrilling effect on him. It wasn't simply her claim about caring that made him half believe her, in spite of his inner warnings to mistrust her entirely; it was that she cared enough to come all the way out here, when few others would have bothered. It was, purely and simply, her.

Trace didn't want to admit that maybe his desire for Jenna Ward went beyond the hard, driving sexual attraction he had for her. That would only complicate things. But even as he thought it, a part of him knew it was too late.

Chapter 3

The day broke clear and dry and hellishly hot. Trace was at work in the main corral with a handsome sorrel gelding. From the saddle he roped a calf from a group of others that huddled against the fence. The horse stepped back to keep the rope taut, restraining the calf. At the subtle tensing of Trace's knees, the horse stepped forward, and the rope slackened. Trace loosed the rope from the calf with a deft flick of the wrist. When the critter turned and ran, the horse sprang into action, interposing itself between the calf and the group, preventing it from returning to the others with the lightning-quick, surefooted maneuvers of an expertly trained cutting horse.

From the corner of his eye, Trace caught a movement by the fence. He didn't have to look in that direction to know that Jenna was there. The horse beneath him felt the imperceptible tensing of Trace's muscles as the air all around him was suddenly charged with electricity.

Trace pulled up on the reins and allowed the calf to return to the group. Then he put the sorrel through its paces. Taught to neck-rein, the big red horse moved away from the pressure of the rein on the opposite side of its neck. It stopped instantly from a gallop at the slightest touch. Ridden one-handed, it went forward at the command of Trace's legs, and stood perfectly still when asked. When it was over, the performance rated a round of applause from Jenna, who stood watching in awe.

Trace knew that he and Teddy were showing off, but so what? It was worth it to see that smile on Jenna's face as he trotted the horse over to where she was standing.

Was it really possible that she got prettier every time he looked at her? And each time she looked at him with those beautiful green eyes, he had to fight down his impulses. If they had lived a hundred years ago, he would simply have thrown her over his horse and ridden off with her. But this was the twentieth century, and he was an Indian, and she was white, and he knew from experience what a deadly combination that could be.

Jenna squinted up at the man who sat astride his horse, looking down at her. Sunlight burst all around from behind him, reflecting off the hard, lean angles of his upper body, spanning the breadth of his shoulders and bouncing like diamonds off his jet-black hair. Stripped naked to the waist, with hair flowing unbound, there was nothing tame about Trace Mc-Call. In some ways, he was as wild as the mustangs he broke. Certainly the feelings he inspired in Jenna were like wild creatures, dangerous and uncontrollable.

"That was wonderful," she said.

Trace slid from the saddle like rainwater and draped the reins loosely over a fence post. "The star of any ranch is a good cutting horse, and Teddy's about as good as they get."

A friendly muzzle poked through the fence at her. "He's beautiful. What kind of horse is he?"

He ran his hand affectionately over the horse's smooth red coat. "Teddy's pure mustang."

He saw the look of surprise that registered on her face and added, "Not all mustangs are like that miserable buckskin. Actually, mustangs are all I train. No stock horse can touch a mustang for cow sense and endurance. Teddy here's more like a sheepdog. He just seems to know what a cow will do next. Whenever I cut yearlings out of a herd, all I have to do is show Teddy the first one. After we bring it out, he goes back and brings out all the others, one by one. Teddy once worked a jackrabbit out of a herd of cattle. A good cutting horse has only to be shown which cow you want and then he does the job himself, even without a bridle."

He spoke in a tone of sharp-edged pride. He clearly loved the horse named Teddy, and it was easy to see he had poured everything he knew into its training.

Jenna couldn't take her eyes from him as he stroked the horse's neck and whispered to it in that language of the Sioux that sounded to her untrained ears so guttural and yet so beautiful at the same time. She was flabbergasted by the tenderness that ran like a crack through his rock-hard demeanor and wondered if he knew how utterly appealing a hint of softness was in a hard-edged man.

"Thanks for the clothes," she said.

Upon waking and finding no one around, Jenna had helped herself to a shower and returned to her room to find a fresh T-shirt and a pair of denim cutoffs neatly laid out on the bed. The clothes were too big to belong to KayCee, so she had naturally assumed it was Trace who had put them there.

To her surprise, he replied, "Don't thank me. I had nothing to do with it."

She felt faint color rise to her cheeks at having thought otherwise. "KayCee?"

"I see she helped herself to a pair of my cutoffs and one of my T-shirts."

"I guess she didn't think you'd mind."

"I don't."

On the contrary, he liked it. He liked it a lot, in fact, seeing Jenna in one of his shirts, looking small-boned and fragile underneath. He didn't mind seeing her in a too-big pair of his cutoffs cinched at the waist with one of his leather belts, either. Whatever objection he might have voiced was overruled by the sudden rush of blood through his veins at the sight of her legs. His guess had been right. They were long, smooth-skinned and shapely. He wondered if the rest of her was as soft to the touch as those legs looked.

Jenna felt herself warming under Trace's stare. "Uh, what exactly do you do here?"

His eyes rose reluctantly, devouring her face with equal intensity. "You just saw some of it. I break and train mustangs. Nobody wants a fiery steed spooking and stampeding the cattle. I train cutting horses to cut, and trail horses to walk or lope slowly alongside a herd, with their heads low, looking bored, so's not to spook the cattle. That sort of thing."

"How do you know which horse will be best for which job?"

"I look for signs. Maybe one is real smart and quick-footed. He'd make a good cutter. Another one's friendly and eager to please. With a little obedience training, he'd make a good pleasure ride. The feisty ones just naturally like to buck, so I sell them to rodeos. The main thing is, a horse has to like what it's doing."

"What are your plans for that buckskin mustang?" she asked.

Trace shook his head thoughtfully. "He's mean, but he's smart and he's quick. If I can train him as a cutter, I can get top dollar for him."

Jenna noticed that Trace seemed more at ease this morning than he had yesterday. He appeared to genuinely like talking about his work, so she used what she suspected was a rare moment of openness in the unapproachable man to poke a little farther beneath the crust of his solitude to the tenderness she sensed was there.

"Horses are a lot like people, aren't they?" she mused. "Some just fight harder for their freedom."

"Freedom doesn't come without a fight," said Trace. "And even then sometimes not at all."

"I think you're being a little cynical."

"That's because you're not an Indian. Read the history books, teacher. My people won every battle they ever fought with the U.S. Army, but they didn't get their freedom. What they got was reservations, poverty and disease." There was no bitterness lacing his words, only a matter-of-fact realism that Jenna found strangely touching.

"Do you ride?" he asked.

"Yes, I do. I spent time on my grandparents' farm when I was young, while my parents battled over me in court."

"Who won?"

"My father."

His eyes brightened with interest. "You were raised by your father?"

"From the age of six."

"Didn't you miss your mother?"

"Terribly. But I got to see her on holidays, and for two weeks every summer."

Which was a hell of a lot more than KayCee had, Trace thought bitterly. With a derisive little snort, he said, "Let me guess. She just walked out one day, right?"

Her dusky voice was soft, almost childlike, when she quietly replied, "Right."

The callousness of his remark hit him like a locomotive. He'd had no idea his sarcasm would be right on target. He wanted to apologize for it and chase away that sad little look that had come over her lovely face, but how could he apologize for his remark without revealing the reason he'd made it? He decided it was better to say nothing at all than to have to explain about Sylvie.

"If she walked out, why'd she fight him in court for custody?"

Jenna lifted her shoulders in a helpless gesture. "She left when I was three. Two years later, she was back. Who knows why? I guess she had her reasons. The bottom line is, she lost, and I went to live with my father."

She couldn't bring herself to tell him about the affair that had rocked her parents' marriage when she was three years old, or to describe the feelings of helplessness and frustration she had experienced, even at that young age, when she couldn't prevent their separating over an issue she didn't understand. There was no way to explain infidelity to a three-year-old.

Years later, when Jenna discovered the reason for her parents' divorce, some quick calculations had brought the whole thing into sharp focus. The fact was, Jenna had been unplanned and unexpected. Her parents had been young, and as young couples sometimes do, they'd found themselves saying hasty *I do*s with a baby on the way. With no real love between them to begin with, they had locked themselves in a loveless union that was doomed from the start.

Jenna had sworn to herself a long time ago that she would not make the same mistake. There would be no one-night stands for her, no wild flings at passion to satisfy a temporary longing. Love wasn't something you dabbled in. It was permanent, irrevocable, forever.

"How'd you like living with your father?"

Trace's voice, cautious but curious, called Jenna back from the bite of childhood memories. Indirectly, she answered, "Little girls are always in love with their fathers. Don't you know that?"

The subject of little girls struck too close to home. Trace turned back to his horse and busied himself with shortening the stirrup, then lengthening it, then setting it back to its original position. "What kind of farm do your grandparents have?"

"It's a dairy farm in upstate New York."

With a laugh, he asked, "What'd you ride? Cows?"

"I'll admit that was some pretty slick work you were doing earlier," said Jenna, "but when it comes to flat-out riding, I'll have you know I can ride as well as you can."

"How'd you like to go for a ride right now?"

"Aren't you busy here?"

"Nope. Teddy's lessons are over for today. I thought I'd give him some exercise. Want to come along?"

"Sure."

"Let me just go tell KayCee that we're going."

He returned a short while later, leading a pretty bay mare. "Do you need a hand up?"

Jenna looked down at the reins draped across his open palm. Annoyed that she had to prove herself to him, she snatched them from his hand and mounted without his assistance, then sat perfectly still, willing her skin not to jump when his hand accidently brushed her legs as he adjusted her stirrups.

The long, flat prairie stretched for as far as the eye could see. In the distance, the Nebraska hills, vibrant and green in the springtime, were drab beneath a hot summer sun. The air was clear and still as they rode, and the wind rustled through the leaves of the cottonwoods. Overhead, a red-backed hawk circled the sky with wings spread on currents of air, its cry piercing the stillness among the clouds.

Without speaking, as if by silent mutual consent, they urged their horses into a trot, then a canter. And then they were galloping across the prairie neck and neck, legs almost touching from horse to horse as they raced toward a grizzled rise in the distance.

With the wind whipping through her hair and her cheeks lashed by the mare's flying mane, Jenna felt an exhilaration unlike anything she'd known since those days when she'd galloped her own horse through the cow pastures of her grandparents' farm.

Crouching low over her horse's neck, she turned her head to look at Trace, astride the horse galloping beside her. His black hair flowed like a mantle behind him. The reins flapped idly while he clenched the coarse black mane in his fists. Dry Nebraska dust was streaked like war paint across his face. For one crazy moment, she thought that this was what he would have looked like if he had ridden into battle a century ago. Even here and now, in the twentieth century, there was something fierce and primal about him as he urged the big red horse ahead of her. His actions were clear. He wasn't about to let her win just because she was a woman. If Jenna wanted this victory, she would have to earn it.

Putting her heels to the mare's flanks, Jenna called out to her, urging the spirited horse faster. The animal responded, closing the gap with each thundering stride.

Trace turned and looked over his shoulder to see Jenna gaining. He knew the mare had speed; he just hadn't counted on Jenna's skill in the saddle. He called some words in Sioux to his mount. The gelding drew away with ever-increasing strides.

It happened fast. One moment the sorrel was flying across the prairie. The next moment he stumbled.

Trace drew up hard on the reins and brought the horse to a halt. Jumping from the saddle, he ran his hands up and down its legs, checking for signs of injury. He should have known better than to race like that across the prairie. He'd seen animals shatter bones stepping in gopher holes. But Teddy hadn't stepped in a hole. He had stumbled of his own accord.

Jenna reined her horse over to them and dismounted. "Are you all right?"

No, damn it, he wasn't all right. If he'd been thinking clearly, this never would have happened, and he wouldn't now be trying to come to grips with the painful fact that Teddy was getting old.

"It's him I'm worried about."

"Is he injured?"

"He's fine, no thanks to you."

"Me? What did I do?"

His dark eyes turned swiftly to meet her questioning ones. "You dared me to race you."

"I didn't dare you to do anything."

"You didn't have to. I'm talking about that look you get in your eyes."

"What look?"

"That look that drives a man crazy."

"Now wait just a minute."

"No, you wait a minute. You waltz out here, looking so damned beautiful and daring me with those eyes, and you don't expect me to react to it? I'm only human, you know. I'm not made out of wood." He thrust his arm out for her inspection. "See? Flesh and blood."

Oh, yes, she could see, all right. She could see the definition of the upper arm that was practically in her face, the broad expanse of naked, heaving chest, the sweat that snaked in tiny rivulets across the smooth, sun-browned skin. The proximity of all that bare masculinity only fueled Jenna's outrage which was already mounting by leaps and bounds.

"I've given you no reason to think that my coming here was for any reason other than strictly professional. And as for your being only human, I'm wondering why you're trying so hard not to show it. All I've seen so far is a temperamental, arrogant, pigheaded man." She pivoted sharply and began to stalk away, but his grip sheathed her arm, preventing her from going anywhere.

In a voice that was both treacherous and thrilling, he drawled, "Really? And I suppose you haven't known from the moment we met that it would lead to this."

"To what? An argument? I can assure you I knew *that* from the start. You're too much like another man I know. Too absorbed in your own self-pity to see the world going by around you. You've locked yourself up inside so tight that nothing can get through, not even your daughter who needs you, the way I needed my father when I was that age. He wasn't there, either."

Jenna was stunned by her own admission. She had never meant to say that. She was so angry that it had spilled out before she could stop it. With the strength of that anger, she tried to pull free of him.

He drew her close, so close that she could feel the warm fan of his breath across her cheek. "No," he said, "not an argument. This."

Without warning, one arm snaked around her waist while the other hand went to the back of her head to splay its fingers in her hair. He pulled her up against him. For several wordless moments, their eyes locked in combat, faces mere inches apart. It wasn't difficult to read the outrage that was aimed at him from those beautiful green eyes. She wasn't about to give freely. He would have to take what he wanted.

His lips came down over hers, obliterating any protest she might have made. There was little tenderness in him, not even a hint of the gentleness he'd exhibited with his horse. He kissed her fiercely, hungrily, overpowering her with the strength in those lean and sinewy muscles.

It was one thing to fantasize about being taken by him. To experience it was another. It was then that Jenna had her first real sense of panic. No, not like this! Not to be taken like a captive against her will, to have her lips plundered and her body pressed painfully against his, without any say in the matter. She fought the restraint of his arms, the bruising pressure of his kiss and the thrust of his swollen arousal. But most of all she fought the unexpected pleasurable sensations that erupted like tiny volcanoes deep inside of her, spreading passion through her system like molten lava.

Trace groaned inwardly and tore his mouth from hers. His chest heaved with the desire that raged like an inferno inside of him. His breath came in hard and rapid bursts as he forced her away to arm's length and held her in his grip to assess the damage. He had to see it for himself. He had to see if she was as affected as he was.

Her lips were red and wet from the ravages of his mouth, her cheeks were flushed with fury, and her breath came in furious little bursts through her nostrils. But her eyes... God, her eyes, blindingly clear in the sunlight, a beautiful green sea in which he saw mirrored the same unbridled passion and frenzied fear that he himself was feeling at this moment.

They stood there like that, neither of them moving, neither of them speaking. And then the sound of Jenna's palm, as it struck Trace's cheek, cracked the air around them.

They rode back to the ranch in acute silence. Jenna was too furious to speak. That kiss had robbed her of her senses for one treacherous moment. She was crazy to have actually liked it. Out of her mind to have half wanted it not to stop. She told herself to forget it, that he was trouble, that he wasn't for her, that the most she could expect from a man like Trace McCall was one night of passion, maybe two. Certainly not the permanent kind of love she dreamed of.

Cursing his impulsive behavior, Trace retreated behind a wall of stony silence. Damn, now he'd really done it. He hadn't meant to feel anything. He'd meant only to take from her the one and only kiss he'd probably ever get. But he'd felt her body tremble and her lips quiver under his, and something had snapped inside him. He had suddenly wanted to possess her—not just her mouth, but all of her. And not in a fit of lust, either, but for a reason that had to do with far more than just her loveliness.

This woman had walked smack-dab into the midst of his daily routine, disrupting his way of thinking, shaking up his emotions, making him remember what it was like to want as fiercely as he found himself wanting her. It wasn't just her beauty that intrigued him. It was the way she refused to be cowed by him. She didn't seem to be at all intimidated, in spite of his efforts to scare her off. On the contrary, she was a gutsy thing, pressing issues when others would have heeded the storm warnings in his eyes and backed off.

Trace had thought he had his life all neatly sewn up. Since Sylvie had walked out, he'd worked from sunup until sundown, throwing himself into the sweat and grit of breaking mustangs to combat the loneliness. It had gotten so that not getting involved had become a way of life for him. It wasn't that the dark-eyed, black-haired beauty of his own kind didn't appeal to him. It was what went beyond the beauty that appealed to a man like Trace. It was the intelligence that brightened a woman's eyes, the proud way she held her body, the movement of her legs, her smile. And when all that walked in on tall, slender legs and looked at him with beautiful emerald eyes, he'd felt his underpinnings beginning to crack.

Whoever would have guessed that someone like Jenna Ward would come along to disturb the sanctity of his self-imposed exile? She was white, forbidden to him by generations of cultural clashes between their two races and by his own past mistakes. Why couldn't she have left him and KayCee alone?

Trace's frown deepened at the thought of KayCee. He lifted a hand and ran it through his hair, sweeping back the long black strands that lay like heavy silk on his cheek, wondering what on earth he was going to do about his daughter.

As they rode through the gate that led back to the stable, a nervous whinny from the corral caught Trace's attention. That miserable buckskin was making a fuss again. He reined Teddy over in that direction to have a look.

The first thing he spotted as he rounded the corner of the stable was an overturned bucket spilling a pile of oats onto the ground. Looking in all directions failed to turn up any sign of KayCee. He was about to call her name when another whinny from the corral, this one high-pitched and dangerous, alarmed him.

Bypassing the stirrup for a quicker dismount, he slung his leg over his horse's shoulders, jumped to the ground and sprinted toward the corral around back, where he stopped dead in his tracks.

The buckskin mustang was pacing back and forth at a nervous gait, hugging the far end of the fence, ears flattened against its head in a distinctly hostile gesture. In the center of the corral stood KayCee, her hand outstretched, a bright red apple sitting on her palm.

Trace felt his extremities turn cold with fear. His impulse was to run to her, scoop her up in his arms and protect her from the attack that was sure to come. But he dared not enter the corral, knowing that doing so would only excite the horse even more. He backed away as slowly and unobtrusively as he could. When he was out of sight of the corral, he turned and raced to the house for his rifle.

When he returned, he froze again, this time with the rifle midway to his shoulder, as he watched Jenna walk slowly and deliberately into the corral.

In a furious whisper through clenched teeth, he demanded, "Are you crazy? Come back here."

But Jenna ignored him, and there was nothing he could do except stand there and watch helplessly, feeling his anxiety mount. He brought the rifle up to his shoulder and caught his target in the sights. With his finger curled around the trigger, he waited, reflexes poised to spring into action.

Jenna entered the corral without looking directly at the buckskin, giving the impression that she didn't even know he was there. Careful to make no sudden movements, she took a few steps forward and stopped. She spoke in a soft, soothing voice.

"KayCee, I want you to back out of the corral as slowly as possible. Whatever you do, honey, don't turn your back on him."

"It's okay, it really is," said KayCee, who turned around in spite of the warning.

Jenna felt her heart stop in her chest. She hadn't thought about helping KayCee when she saw her in the corral with that horse; she'd acted without thinking. Now, for the first time she was cognizant of her actions. Having been taught never to turn her back on an angry horse, Jenna was certain they were both doomed now.

But the anticipated attack never came. The buckskin moved in a trot up and down the length of the fence, keeping his distance. When Jenna finally did look at him, she saw that his ears were up and pricked forward. He was ever so aware of them, and perhaps even a little bit curious.

"See?" KayCee's voice fairly chirped with satisfaction. "He likes me."

Far from convinced, Jenna cautiously approached the girl and took her by the hand.

KayCee protested, "But I haven't given him the apple yet."

"Fine. Let's just leave it right here on the ground, and he can decide if he wants it." Slowly but surely she and KayCee backed out of the corral.

Trace couldn't believe what he had just witnessed. Relieved and furious at the same time, he didn't know whether to hug his daughter or scold her. And Jenna! Damn her for that harebrained stunt she'd just pulled. Did either of them have any idea how much they'd scared him? He stormed forward, rifle in hand, looking as if he would explode with fury.

KayCee bit her bottom lip and mumbled under her breath, "Uh-oh."

Jenna stepped forward. "Now, Trace—"

"Keep out of this, Jenna."

"Trace, you can see that nothing happened."

"All I see is one crazy woman who's lucky to be alive. And you—" His anger-filled gaze shifted to his daughter. "Didn't I tell you to stay away from that horse?"

"But, Dad, he was about to take the apple right out of my hand." Not even her father's fury, or the prospect of a stiff punishment, could dim the girl's excitement.

"Damn it, KayCee, you're lucky you still *have* a hand."

"But—"

"No buts. I'm telling you, KayCee, stay away from that horse. And stop looking at me that way. You'd think he was your best friend or something. That horse would sooner kill you than not."

"Buck wouldn't do that," the girl said petulantly.

Jenna spoke up in an attempt to shift Trace's anger away from KayCee. "Why do you call him Buck, KayCee? Is it because of his color?"

KayCee's bottom lip jutted out. She looked to be on the verge of tears. Yet, with a hint of the arrogance she had inherited from her hot-tempered father, she replied, "No. Because he bucks my dad off all the time."

Trace stood there looking angry and embarrassed. Against her will, Jenna's heart went out to him. For all his strength and pride, he looked like a man in trouble. More than once she had glimpsed the expression of helplessness that flashed across his face whenever KayCee was mentioned, and she recognized the loneliness that showed at times when he thought no one was watching. He seemed to be at war within himself over something, and it was clear from the look on his face at this moment that he was losing the battle.

Chapter 4

The door to the schoolhouse yawned open and children spilled out like ants from a disturbed mound, their high-pitched laughter filling the barren yard. When the last child had skipped off for recess, a tall, lean figure stepped out into the sunshine.

With a sweep of her hand, Jenna brushed her heavy hair up off her shoulders. The air was hot against the damp skin of her neck, but the breeze that blew constantly quickly evaporated the beads of moisture that dotted her skin. Sunlight skimmed across her hair, highlighting the chestnut locks in varying shades of gold as they tumbled back to her shoulders. Taking a few moments to unwind, she leaned against the building, palms splayed over the rough-hewn planks, and turned her face toward the sun.

It had been a hectic day so far. One student had blackened another student's eye. And Billy Hobbs was complaining that another apple had been stolen from his lunch box. KayCee, she thought with a sigh. What was she going to do about KayCee? Jenna's heart went out to her, for she knew from experience just how tragically hopeless divorce could make a child feel.

It couldn't be easy for Trace, either. Dealing with a daughter on the verge of puberty had to be a father's worst nightmare. She could recall the helpless and impatient look she'd seen on her own father's face when she was KayCee's age. Whenever he was around, that is. She could have forgiven his lack of attention, if only she'd had his physical presence to reassure her that everything would be all right.

Trace McCall wasn't a perfect father, but at least he was there. Despite his arrogance and pigheadedness, she sensed a bond between Trace and KayCee that went beyond their being father and daughter. It was because they were Indians first and all else second, and because it was easy to see that Trace loved his daughter.

Jenna shivered in spite of the sun that turned her skin slowly browner, for something told her that he was the kind of man who, when he loved, loved fiercely. Again she found herself wondering what it would be like to be loved by him. Would it be that all-consuming you-can-never-turn-back kind of love, or something quick, fleeting, like the thrill of a roller coaster, gone soon after the ride was over?

She pushed the thought aside and sought to concentrate on nothing at all, but her thoughts kept straying to the dark-eyed Santee. All around her, children ran and skipped and shouted, but with her eyes closed to the soothing ministrations of the sun, all Jenna could think of was his kiss.

In all her life, she'd never been kissed like that, so impersonally and yet so thoroughly. There had been no gentleness in it, no enticement to kiss him back. He had kissed her harshly, as if to punish her for something that wasn't her fault, without any care as to whether she liked it or not. She had suspected that he would feel like that, all strong-muscled and hot-breathed, but she hadn't anticipated the sheer forcefulness with which he would take what he wanted. In those furious few seconds, he had given her a glimpse of something that both excited and frightened her, and left her to wonder how it was possible to dislike a man as much as she disliked Trace McCall and yet thrill to the punishing taste of his lips.

From where he stood, with one booted foot propped up on the chrome bumper of his pickup, Trace watched her every movement. A gesture as simple as sweeping the hair up off her neck was unexpectedly provocative, because she was so unaware of the sensuality of it. He watched helplessly as she braced one foot on the wall behind her and the hem of her skirt slid to the side to expose one long, slender leg. His muscles tensed at the sight of her profile etched against the blue panorama. She was even more beautiful than he remembered, exuding that lazy sexuality that had been preying on his mind for days now.

As she basked in the warm South Dakota sunshine, thinking unsettling thoughts, an inexplicable sensation began to creep over Jenna. Something made her open her eyes and turn her head. She tensed to find those exquisite black eyes fixed on her with startling intensity from across the schoolyard.

She pushed herself away from the schoolhouse and approached, thinking dismally that this must be what quicksand was like. She smiled and held out her hand and said, "Good morning."

He wasn't surprised by the strength in her grip. He'd felt her power when she slapped him. To his chagrin, she inquired, "How's the cheek?"

He rubbed the place where her angry palm had made contact with his face, and said with grudging appreciation, "That's some wallop you pack."

Jenna's own cheeks colored at the reminder of the kiss that had prompted the slap. "What brings you here today?"

"You left something at the house." He thrust a hand into the pocket of his cowhide vest and pulled out the fabric belt to the dress she had worn the other day. It dangled from his palm, its ends flicked about by the breeze.

Jenna took it gingerly. "You didn't have to come all the way across the river just to return my belt."

"I didn't. I'm taking KayCee to her grandmother's for dinner."

She felt foolish for having thought he had used the belt as an excuse to come all the way across the river to see her. In some crazy way, she was actually disappointed. Hastily she balled up the belt and stuffed it in the pocket of her skirt.

"If you have a long way to go, I can let KayCee go early," she offered.

"That won't be necessary. My mother only lives about twelve miles from here."

"Do you see her often?"

"Every couple of weeks or so."

She was struck by the thought that he had been so close on several occasions, and she hadn't known it. She asked herself what difference it would have made if she had known, but she didn't have an answer for that.

"School's not out for another couple of hours," she said.

He stared at her, his gaze narrowed against the dry summer wind. "That's all right, I'll wait."

"You might as well come inside, then. It's a little cooler, with all the fans going."

They turned and walked toward the schoolhouse together.

"I didn't take your stupid apple!"

Their heads spun in unison at the sound of Kay-Cee's voice.

KayCee stood toe-to-toe with Billy Hobbs in the middle of the schoolyard. Although she was a good head shorter than the fourteen-year-old, the fists that were balled at her sides looked about to fly into action.

Jenna took a step forward to head off the inevitable, but Trace's grip on her forearm stopped her.

She looked at him disbelievingly. "Don't tell me you're going to let her fight that boy. Is that how you expect her to grow up to be strong and independent? We both know she took the apple, Trace."

"You're wrong, teacher. I wasn't about to let her get pummeled by that kid. Let me handle it." His expression showed his barely restrained anger as he moved past her and strode toward his daughter.

From the distance, Jenna watched the two of them as they stood talking for several minutes in the crowded schoolyard. From the looks on KayCee's unsmiling face and Trace's scowling one, it was easy to see that unpleasant words were passing between them.

When Trace returned, Jenna said to him, "It might help if you bought some apples."

Her unsolicited humor brought a look of sharp annoyance. "I told you before, KayCee doesn't eat apples."

"No, but Buck does."

"Don't remind me," he said with a groan. "Besides, we weren't talking about the apple. She wants to go to that damned rodeo. She's been pestering me about it all week."

"So, take her."

"I can't do that. I told you—"

"Yes, you told me. You have to work." She pivoted on her heel and went inside.

He followed her into the building, complaining, "You don't understand."

At her desk, Jenna stacked some papers, giving the edges angry little pats. "I understand that a little bit of your time would go a long way in healing what's ailing KayCee. And she obviously has her heart set on going to that rodeo. I thought a man like you would enjoy the excitement of a rodeo.''

She talked about going to the rodeo as if it were as simple as that, but Trace knew better. His voice was low and belligerent when he spoke from across the room. "How do you know what a man like me would enjoy?''

"You break mustangs, don't you?''

Those obsidian eyes narrowed upon her face. "So?''

It wasn't just what he did for a living that made Jenna think he would feel at home amid the dust and danger of the rodeo. It was also the uncompromising look in his eyes, even now, from across the room, with the sunshine slanting across his face from an open window, telling her that he was the kind of man who lived and loved hard. Her throat went dry. If it was possible to feel consumed by a stare alone, that was how she felt.

Caught in his gaze, the anger he had piqued in her drained. "You just seem to be the type who likes all that action. But if the rodeo's not your thing . . . ''

The bell rang, relieving Jenna of the awkward silence that followed. She cleared her throat, and told him, "You can take a seat at the back of the room.''

For the next hour and a half, Jenna did her best to ignore the man whose six-foot frame was scrunched into the small chair behind the equally small desk at the back of the classroom. Somehow she made it through world history and math. Thankfully, the clock above the blackboard on the wall signaled only a few minutes left. Finally the bell rang and the children all raced out of the building.

Jenna tucked some papers into a leather briefcase and walked outside with Trace.

"Can we give you a lift somewhere?" he asked. His hair was like jet, smooth and sleek and glinting from the sharp glare of the sun, and his eyes were like rocks, hard and unrelenting, betrayed only by the faintly veiled eagerness with which he asked the question.

"No thanks. My car's just over there." She pointed to a foreign model sitting in the shade of a cottonwood, not far from where KayCee was waiting beside Trace's pickup.

"Are you hungry?" Trace asked KayCee as they approached.

KayCee nodded.

"Let's go, then." He turned to get into the pickup, but a tug on his sleeve brought him back around. He bent forward so that KayCee could whisper something in his ear.

He looked at her closely and asked, "Are you sure?"

Another nod.

"Well, go on, then, ask her."

KayCee cast a hesitant look over at Jenna and approached tentatively, no longer looking like the same little girl who could knock Billy Hobbs's block off.

"Would you like to come with us?"

Jenna was caught off guard by the invitation. "Well, I . . . I . . ."

"Grandma makes real good ribs."

An apprehensive glance at Trace's impassive face showed little assistance offered there. "I'll bet she does."

The prospect of having dinner with them brought with it a surge of anxiety, for Jenna already knew how nerve-racking it was to be in Trace McCall's presence. Something about that man positively unhinged her. But how could she refuse the invitation without having it misconstrued by KayCee as rejection? Feeling selfish for thinking only of herself, Jenna forced her misgivings aside and said, "If you're sure your grandmother won't mind."

KayCee's face lit up like a pinball machine. "She won't, right, Dad?"

Trace gave a stiff nod in reply.

Jenna bit a corner of her lip and inquired, "And your dad? Are you sure it's all right with him?"

"Oh, he said he didn't think it was such a good idea."

That would explain the grave look on Trace's face when KayCee had been whispering in his ear, and suddenly Jenna realized that if her presence at dinner bothered anyone, it was him. In her mind she manufactured a dozen excuses for backing out of the invitation, but the smile on KayCee's face rejected each one of them, and all she could think of to say was "I'll follow you there in my car."

Trace had watched their exchange with a mixture of amusement and panic. He had wondered while driving over here today whether she would have the same impact on him one week after she had barged uninvited into his life. The answer was a resounding yes—and then some.

The natural beauty that had stolen his breath away the first time was only enhanced by the rosy blush that covered her face, caused in part by the sun, but mostly, he knew, by KayCee's invitation, which, frankly, had surprised the hell out of him, too.

"The roads are rough," he said. "We're better off taking the pickup. Where do you live?"

"About five miles west of here."

The wind picked up a strand of jet-black hair and blew it across his face as he turned his head to scan the dust-filled horizon, where one lonely road ran east and west in the distance.

"You're on the way. We'll follow you to your place. You can drop off your car, and we'll take the pickup."

Fifteen minutes later, Jenna was seated in the pickup, with Trace stoic behind the wheel, KayCee seated between them, bouncing down the rutted road that led to his mother's house.

They drove past the tired agency town, which was a study in disrepair. In the distance were fields of wheat and potatoes and herds of white-faced steers fenced in on the rolling plains that had once been home to millions of buffalo.

At the edge of one small community stood the small frame house of Mary Bearheels McCall.

With her face deeply seamed from decades beneath the scorching prairie sun, the woman who greeted them at the door looked older than her years. Jenna felt the calluses on the dark-skinned hand that reached out to shake hers when Trace performed the introductions. There was caution in the small black eyes that regarded Jenna closely, and suspicion in her hushed tone when she turned quickly to Trace and muttered something in their own language.

She showed them into a living room that was small and free of unnecessary clutter. A worn brown sofa sat before a stone fireplace, its frayed arms covered with crocheted doilies. A recliner that had seen better days faced the screen of a small television whose antenna held a wad of aluminum foil at its tip for better reception. There was a table with four chairs that didn't match, and a lamp with a yellowed pleated shade. The furnishings were inviting in their shabbiness, as if each piece, like its owner, had many stories to tell.

KayCee was right about the ribs. They were delicious, cooked over an open flame with red potatoes and onions, and served with generous portions of grease bread, a biscuit dough fried in deep fat. KayCee chattered away during the meal, mostly to her grandmother. The old woman's relationship with the young girl appeared open and relaxed. If KayCee was unhappy, it wasn't because of a lack of love, Jenna decided as she casually observed them during the meal.

"Dinner was delicious, Mrs. McCall," she said when she finished eating and pushed her plate away. "I know now why KayCee's stew was so good."

Mary looked questioningly at Trace.

"Jenna had dinner with us one night last week," he explained. "The ferry broke down, and she spent the night." He saw the imperceptible flaring of his mother's eyes as apprehension darted through them, yet he saw no reason to lie to her. He knew his mother was wary of Jenna because she was white. *Washichu.* That was the word she had whispered to him earlier. One word, but it had been enough to make a point. She'd been warning him to be careful.

Jenna saw the look that passed between mother and son. It wasn't hard to figure out that her presence made the Indian woman uneasy, or to understand why. In the months she'd been here, she had learned that some of the Sioux, particularly the old-timers, were leery of accepting strangers into their midst.

Determined to be accepted for who she was and not what she was, Jenna worked hard to put their minds at ease. Often she drove miles out of her way to visit parents who lived in remote areas. Although most of them spoke English, she had taken the time to learn a few words in their own language to make them feel more comfortable. She understood, for example, the word Trace's mother had whispered earlier through gritted teeth.

Jenna didn't like being labeled, but she tolerated it, for she knew just how powerful grandparents were among the Sioux, not only within the family, but within the tribe, as well. They were the keepers of the stories and the myths, the ones who taught the history and traditions of the people as tools for survival. In spite of decades of hardscrabble existence, the reason the tribes continued to exist at all was because of women like Mary Bearheels McCall, who kept the traditions alive.

Turning to KayCee, who was happily eating her dessert of canned peaches, Jenna said, "You must hear some wonderful stories from your grandmother."

Mary looked up, surprised that the white woman was so knowledgeable about their ways. Unbidden, she said, "I can recall the stories my mother told of the summer camp of her childhood, on the edge of the Black Hills. More than thirty tepees were set up. There was Red Leaf, the leader. Fall, her paternal grandfather. Her uncle White Crow, and her father's cousin next to him, and another relative named Little Deer."

She rattled off the names as if she had known them personally, the stories told to her as important as the ones she told KayCee around a warm winter fire. She said something to Trace, who got up and went inside. Minutes later, he returned with what appeared to be a blanket over his arms.

The smell of mildew wrinkled Jenna's nose when he unfurled it over the floor. It wasn't a blanket at all, but the hide of a buffalo, the hair still thick and cinnamon brown on one side, the smooth side painted with brightly colored pictographs.

"It's a winter count," said Mary. "The years are titled, not numbered. This is my great-grandfather's count, begun by his grandfather in 1807." She bent over and ran her hand reverently over the smooth tanned hide.

Among the myriad scenes depicted there was a meteor shower, a tepee burning, horses being stolen from the Crows, a fight with the Pawnees. For the next hour Jenna sat spellbound as the old woman took her on a journey through Lakota history, to times that were richly embedded in her mind through the drawings of her ancestors. The last entry told of the first Sioux dance lodge made of logs.

"That one is called He Dog Band Made a Dance Hall," Mary explained. "Eighteen eighty-three. It stops there."

Jenna was taken with the primitive beauty of the hide, but also perplexed. "It's strange that there's no mention of battles with the U.S. Army," she observed. "Not even the victory over Custer."

"Your textbooks don't make much mention of our history," said Mary. "Why should we concern ourselves with yours? What you see here is what my people consider the important events in their lives—the loss of a leader, the hardship of a cruel winter, intertribal warfare. This is *our* history, not yours."

"And yet our histories are so entwined," said Jenna. "You'd think the winter counts and the history books could both get it right."

Mary smiled and nodded. "Ah, *tokala.*"

"My mother called you a fox," said Trace. "I'm inclined to agree." He smiled that rare smile of his, the one with the power to take her breath away.

Mary saw it and realized that her son was beyond saving. "I will make the tea." She got up and went into the kitchen where she brewed a pot of tea made from cherry-tree bark, while contemplating the woman in the other room who produced such a visible effect on her son.

Raised in the old way, practicing the ceremonies of the Sioux and clinging to ancient Indian beliefs, Mary had initially mistrusted Jenna, but she was beginning to waver. She was impressed by the white woman's eagerness to learn, and touched by what appeared to be a genuine liking for Trace, a liking Mary could see that she was trying hard not to show. This one, Mary sensed, was different.

Just then Trace's voice rose, angry and loud, from the other room, followed by the slamming of the screen door. Mary closed her eyes and shook her head. Were her son and granddaughter arguing again? It seemed some things never changed.

She grasped a frayed pot holder, removed the pot from the stove and poured the steaming tea into only two of the cups she'd taken from the cupboard. She left the third cup empty, knowing her son would be back for it when he was ready.

With the two cups of tea in her hands, she started for the door, which was partly ajar, but paused at the sound of voices from the next room, Jenna's sounding smooth and calming compared to KayCee's, which was on the verge of breaking.

"Why is he being like that?" KayCee whined. "Crandall's only fifty miles away."

Her eyes were blurred by tears and her bottom lip quivered, and although she was trying hard to sound merely angry, she was devastated.

"I'm sure he didn't mean it. Maybe you could speak to him about it again in the morning." Jenna tried to sound hopeful, despite Trace's flat refusal to take KayCee to the rodeo.

"You heard him. I can't go and that's it."

"KayCee, honey," she said gently, "did it ever occur to you that if he says no, maybe he has a reason?"

"Sure. His reason's Mom. She's gonna be there, and he doesn't want me to see her."

Suddenly it all made sense. What Trace was trying so hard to hide spilled from his daughter's lips with unwitting ease. It was worse than Jenna had imagined. And hauntingly familiar.

"When was the last time you saw your mother?"

KayCee replied between sniffles, "I don't know. Maybe it's been a year."

To a child, a year was like forever. No wonder KayCee wanted so badly to go to the rodeo. And no wonder Trace, steeped in his own bitterness, refused to let her go.

If Trace didn't want to see his ex-wife, that was understandable, but why deny KayCee the opportunity to see her mother? Jenna patted the girl's hand affectionately and said, "Would you like to go with me?"

A smile made a brave attempt to break through the tears. "If my dad lets me."

"If I let you what?"

Jenna and KayCee looked up from their private conversation to see Trace's tall, shadowy figure behind the screen door. KayCee bit her lip and said, "I was thinking of spending the night with Grandma. Is it okay?"

The hinges squeaked when the door swung open and he came inside. "Sure. Why wouldn't it be?"

"No reason. Just asking." She got up and quickly disappeared into the kitchen, but not before giving Jenna a conspiratorial look.

"Let me guess," he said. "You're supposed to work on me."

"Not at all," Jenna replied. "Although now I think I understand why you're so dead set against taking her to the rodeo."

"You think you understand, huh?" There was a belligerent challenge in his tone of displeasure.

"It has to do with your ex-wife, right?"

It had never been his nature to lie when the truth would do just as well. Yet neither was he about to open up that can of worms. He replied curtly, "Right."

"That's why I offered to take her myself."

"You what?"

"If it's all right with you, that is."

"It's *not* all right with me. What right do you have to—" He bit off the rest of his words when his mother appeared in the doorway with three cups of tea on a tray. She gave him a harsh look, warning him not to press the issue.

It took every ounce of willpower Trace possessed to respect his mother's wish and keep silent when he really wanted to tell Jenna to mind her own business. And yet he could also almost imagine telling her everything. It was crazy, he knew, but she did that to him, muddling his senses with that smooth-skinned beauty and provoking nature of hers.

A powerful emotion came and went quickly in Trace's dark eyes as he sat down again at the table from which he had stormed a short while before, having nearly knocked his chair over backward in the process.

When he had drained his cup of the last drop of tea, he said tersely, "It's late. We should be going."

At the door, he watched in amazement as his mother's hand curled affectionately around Jenna's. Behind them, KayCee chirped an uncharacteristically friendly good-night. Their liking of Jenna only made it harder for him to resist her. He was feeling outnumbered as he slid his lean frame behind the steering wheel and started the engine.

Chapter 5

A charged silence filled the cab of the pickup, broken only by the hum of the engine as they bumped their way down the narrow access road.

Jenna spoke up tentatively, testing her voice against the silence. "I want to thank you for inviting me to your mother's today."

"Thank KayCee. It was her idea."

"I know that. But I also know it wouldn't have happened if you didn't say it was all right."

He drove with his eyes glued to the road, without responding.

He was trying to assess just how much she knew. Whatever she had learned from KayCee, she couldn't know how afraid he was of losing his daughter, because KayCee herself didn't know. Not that he expected Sylvie to want KayCee back, but then, he hadn't expected Sylvie to actually leave in the first place. And although he had learned over the course of his life to take what he wanted, he had also learned to take nothing for granted.

"KayCee adores you, you know."

Jenna's voice called him back from the painful possibility of the thing he feared the most. "You could have fooled me."

The subject of the rodeo had come up at the table and words had flared suddenly between him and KayCee. It had been like what happens to a simmering cooking fire when a piece of fat is dropped into it.

"Oh, Trace, she wants so much to go. She thinks you're being unreasonable." She paused, then added, almost apologetically, "I can't say I blame her."

The air inside the pickup grew thicker with tension as Trace took the curves of the dark and lonely road.

Jenna laid her head back against the seat and turned her head toward the window to watch the landscape fly by in a series of dark, undulating shadows against the night.

Trace's stony gaze left the road, to settle on the woman sitting beside him. The night wind blew her hair about her face. With her head tilted back, the smooth white skin of her throat looked like alabaster in the moonlight.

Why did she have to be sitting there like that, looking so beautiful, tying his stomach into painful knots with sheer longing for her? Her voice was smooth and husky and desperately alluring when it drifted into the stillness between them.

"I remember what it was like. My father hated my mother. He never had the time for me, but he couldn't stand it whenever I saw her. I didn't understand it, of course. All I knew was that she was my mother, and as much as it hurt when she left, I still loved her just as much."

"You think I hate my ex-wife?" he said roughly.

"*Hate*'s a strong word. *Resent,* maybe?"

With a derisive snort, he exclaimed, "Damn right I resent her. But I don't hate her. Sylvie's just like the rest of us. We just can't help being who we are."

She peered at him through the darkness. "If you believe that, then why can't you believe how important it is for KayCee to see her mother?"

A stop sign suddenly loomed at the intersection with the state road up ahead. He braked hard, and the pickup slid to a halt. The engine idled as he turned to look at her. His eyes were bright and beautiful in the starlight, and his face was flushed with dusky color.

"Did anyone ever tell you that you ask too many questions?"

"Yes, my father, when I used to ask him when my mother was coming home."

He exhaled a breath of impatience. "Sylvie's not coming home."

"Maybe you need to tell that to KayCee. Be honest with her, Trace. Tell her the real reason you don't want her to see her mother."

A muscle twitched at the corner of his mouth, pulling it downward into a frown. "And what reason would that be?"

"Beats me," she said. "It could be any number of things. Maybe you're still in love with her." Inwardly Jenna was aghast. How had she dared to suggest such a thing? And yet her breath stuck in her throat as she waited for his reply.

"Hell, I stopped loving Sylvie a long time ago." He plunged the gearshift into first and peeled onto the main road with a screech of tires.

How was it that she was able to do this to him? She had a way of pulling things out of him, like feelings he didn't know he had and words he never expected to say. But then, she'd been full of surprises ever since he met her, like the way she'd walked bravely into the corral to rescue KayCee, and the easy and unaffected way she had charmed his mother without even trying. He'd never meant to tell her about Sylvie, but somehow it wasn't as hard as he'd have thought it would be, when the night was still and the road was dark and it was Jenna who was doing the listening.

"We've been divorced for five years. She was the one who wanted out. The lure of the rodeo was just too great to keep her here."

"Lots of women have careers," said Jenna. "Couldn't she have tried hers and still remained married?"

"She did, at first. When the competition was local, we used to pack up KayCee and take her along. But Sylvie's good at what she does. Pretty soon she made a name for herself and began spending more and more time away from home. Things got pretty bad after that. In the end, I told her she'd have to make a choice—her career or KayCee." He saw the look of astonishment on Jenna's face and said adamantly, "The rodeo circuit's no place to bring up a kid."

But Jenna's astonishment was not caused by the painful choice Trace had given his ex-wife. Her voice echoed her disbelief when she exclaimed, "She gave up custody?"

"Sylvie's a small-town girl with big-time ambitions. She doesn't belong in a place like this."

"Still, it couldn't have been easy for her."

"Easy or not, she did it." He snorted derisively at the bitter memory. "I have this crazy notion that you just don't walk out of a marriage like you were walking out of a drugstore."

"Does she keep in touch with KayCee?"

"She calls once in a while from wherever she happens to be. Sometimes she sends pictures."

"KayCee said it's been about a year since she saw her."

"I let my mother take her to the rodeo in Crandall last year."

"Why not let your mother take her again?"

"Because KayCee came back real upset. I had to sit up with her at night while she cried herself to sleep."

"Yes, I remember that part, too," said Jenna, her voice reflective, as the memory came back, as clear as day. "I used to come home and cry my eyes out. It wasn't that I wanted my parents to get back together again. They spent their married years in a state of war, so I knew that wasn't going to happen. And it wasn't that I wanted to live with my mother, either, because I still resented her for abandoning us. I think now it was because there was nothing I could do about any of it. I can remember feeling so small and helpless."

The memories caught up with her, plunging her into painful remembering, and she was unaware that they had come to a halt and that Trace had shut off the engine.

He rested his elbow on the back of the seat and leaned his head against his palm as he studied her. In a low voice, he said, "You don't strike me as the helpless type. That means there's hope for KayCee."

His expression was no longer belligerent. In the moonlight that slashed across his face, Jenna saw something that frightened her even more. It was desire, simmering deep in his eyes, like lights from distant fires.

She smiled halfheartedly. "I've done all right for myself. But it hasn't been easy. Besides, KayCee's different. She might not be so lucky."

He ran his hand through his hair, sweeping the black locks from his eyes with a tired gesture. "What if I let her go and...and Sylvie..." It was hard enough just thinking it, and even harder voicing the possibility. And Jenna wasn't making it any easier, with that vulnerable look in her eyes and that half-pleading quaver in her voice.

His own voice sounded angry and desperate when he blurted out, "Damn it, Jenna, what if Sylvie wants her back?"

Through the darkness, she thought she saw a glimmer of fear race across that handsome, hard-boned face, and suddenly she understood the real cause of his refusal to let KayCee go to the rodeo.

"I know what it's like to be on KayCee's end," she said, "but I can only guess what it's been like for you. Still, Trace, the court awarded you custody, didn't it?"

"The tribal court, you mean. Sylvie abided by it because she knows how influential the council can be. But what if she sues for custody in the U.S. courts?"

"She didn't do that the last time she saw KayCee. Why would she do it now?"

He looked strongly into her questioning eyes and voiced his growing fear. "How do I know why Sylvie does anything? What if she sees the great kid KayCee is growing into and wants her back?"

She wanted to tell him that everything would be all right, but she knew that life didn't always work out that way. All she could do was share with him a bit of her own childhood pain, in the hope that he would understand his daughter's, and tell him, in a softly apologetic tone, "If you don't risk anything, you won't get anything back."

Somehow, she made everything so clear. And so inevitable. There was no escaping what Trace knew he had to do.

"Okay, she can go," he said. "Is that what you want to hear?"

"It's a start," she conceded. "Will you take her?"

He drew in a deep, uncertain breath and let it out through pursed lips. "I will, on one condition—that you come with us."

She looked away from the eagerness she saw in his eyes. "Me? But why?"

"KayCee is comfortable with you, I can tell. It's bound to be a difficult day for her, and having you there just might make it easier. And since you offered to take her yourself..."

"All right, all right. If it will be of some help to KayCee, I'll go with you." Her hand fumbled with the door latch in the darkness as she let herself out.

Trace was out of the pickup and at her side before both her feet touched the ground. There was a fierce glow in his eyes when he gestured past her, toward the house, and ventured, "Do you live alone?"

Jenna's voice scratched at the back of her throat. "Yes."

"I'll wait until you're inside."

"All right."

But neither of them moved.

"Go," he urged, his voice ragged. "Now. Because I warn you, Jenna, once I have you, I'll never let you go."

He smelled of musk and desire, and Jenna's pulse soared.

"You sound serious," she said, trying to look unconcerned, when in fact she was shaking uncontrollably inside.

"I'm a serious man, Jenna, when it comes to something I want."

An inner voice screamed for Jenna to run, but she stood rooted to the spot, unable to move beneath the scrutiny of those dark eyes. Somehow, when she wasn't looking, this man had slipped beneath her guard.

"You're big on truth, aren't you, Jenna? Here's some truth for you." His dangerous drawl should have warned her of what was coming next. "I want you, naked and ready under me. More than I thought I could want a woman."

His warm, moist breath whispered against the night, sending chills down Jenna's spine. "I've been thinking about it from the first moment I saw you."

Jenna was more wildly afraid than she'd ever been in her life. To be wanted by a man with such fierce desire was one thing, but to want him back with the same overwhelming emotion was something new and frightening to her.

Desire conflicted sharply with logic. Could she compromise everything she believed about love for a night of passion with Trace McCall? It would have been so easy for her to give in to him, if only for tonight... and if only she were a different person.

Her voice was low and unsteady. "Trace...I...I can't."

He gave an abrupt laugh to camouflage the disappointment that tore through him. "Right," he said gruffly. "But maybe you'd better know what you're up against."

Automatically his arms closed around her, practically lifting her off her toes.

His body was lean and firm and incredibly strong, the way she remembered it from that day out on the prairie. With her breasts crushed against his chest, she could feel the savage pounding of his heart.

Or was that her own heart, beating like a war drum in her chest, sending its rhythm clear to her brain?

"You're so beautiful, Jenna," he murmured against her hair. "And I've been very patient. But there's a limit to what I can take." With increasing urgency, he pulled her up harder against him. "Kiss me," he whispered, his voice a hoarse groan. "Just this once, Jenna. Kiss me."

She was in his head, in his blood, and it was suddenly no longer enough to take kisses from her by force. He wanted one back, willingly, with the same desperation he himself was feeling at that very moment. He wanted to feel her breath mingling with his and the tickle of her tongue in his mouth. He wanted to hear her breathless voice at his ear, to feel the eager exploration of her hands. He wanted to know that she wanted him as much as he wanted her.

His eyes were so fiery-bright that it almost hurt to look at him through the moonlit darkness. Jenna closed her eyes against their impact. She could feel the muscles flexing in his arms as he slid his hands downward over her hips to familiarize himself with the curves and hollows of her body. A shudder of pure excitement raced through her at the scrape of his calluses across the fabric of her skirt. Here was a man with raw and intense power, a man who worked and loved equally hard, a man who could protect a woman from everything except herself.

He brought one hand up to her neck, where his thumb came to rest upon the erratically beating pulse at her throat. His heated gaze followed a wisp of chestnut hair as it curled against her throat and rested upon the heaving curve of her breasts.

"Kiss me, Jenna."

A faint sigh of surrender spilled from her lips. Her hands slid up his smoothly muscled arms and across his shoulders, twining at the back of his neck, where his hair was as soft and sleek as silk in her grasping fingers. Her head tilted back, lips parted to receive his kiss.

Unlike that first kiss out on the prairie, this one was aflame with equal passion, and the shared ardor of two lonely and confused people. The kiss deepened, and a wild longing surged through Jenna, spreading like liquid heat right down to her fingertips. So easy, she thought helplessly. So easy...

But deep within her consciousness, a small voice struggled to be heard, begging her not to take leave of her senses. Things were moving much too fast. What would one kiss accomplish, except to shatter her illusions about love being more than just a one-night stand?

Trace felt Jenna's hands between them, gently pushing him away, and he knew that one kiss was all he was going to get. In a low growl of suppressed emotion, he told her, "I want you, but I'm not about to beg for it."

Jenna's heart was thudding in the strained silence that followed. She wanted to say something, *any*-thing, to chase that look of pained disappointment away from his face. And to banish these feelings of guilt, for the truth of it was, she had wanted him to kiss her. Had wanted to feel his mouth on hers. Had longed for the sheer physical strength of his arms around her. But that didn't change who she was or what she was all about.

She drew a breath of warm, sultry air into her lungs for support. When she spoke, her words were low, barely uttered against the dark heat of the night. "I'm not the kind of woman who does things halfway, Trace. If it's a one-night stand you're looking for, you'll have to look somewhere else."

The darkness could not conceal the look of blasted expectation on his handsome face, or quell the burning fires that raged within Jenna. To her regret, she found that turning Trace away at her door was one of the hardest things she had ever had to do.

Chapter 6

The summer air sizzled with the smell of horseflesh and cotton candy. With the opening grand entry of all the participants, the frontier spirit of the old West came to life.

From his seat in the stands, Trace's dark eyes swept the arena, searching for one face in particular. He had come today to do battle, a reluctant warrior amid the pageantry of the rodeo.

Trace's eyes moved like a predator's, sifting through the dust kicked up by hundreds of parading hooves. Where was the sequined outfit that reflected the glare of the sun, and the trademark white Stetson from beneath which flew her mane of golden hair? Where was that one face out of all the others that would determine the outcome of this day, and possibly the future?

She was nowhere in sight. He sighed deeply, the sound swallowed up by the cheering crowd. Relief swarmed over him. The muscles that had been tied in knots all morning began to unwind. He sat back against the hard bleacher seat, Jenna on one side of him, KayCee on the other, feeling for the first time today a sense of excitement stirred up by the rodeo, by KayCee's smiling face and by Jenna's long-lashed eyes, looking greener and more beautiful in the warm sunshine than he'd ever seen them.

The first event was the chuck-wagon races, in which teams of horses pulled Conestoga wagons around the track at madcap speeds. Trace hardly noticed the frantic activity in the arena, with Jenna sitting so close to him and the fragrance of her hair carried on the wind and penetrating his senses. It was impossible to prevent his thoughts slipping back to the other night, when he had felt himself skyrocketing in her arms.

She had surprised him by kissing him when he asked for it. In that brief moment, when their breath mingled and her hands were clasped around his neck and he could feel the gentle play of her fingers in his hair, he had known that she wanted it as much as he did. Yet she had surprised him again by pushing him away and denying the frenzied need that had consumed them both, offering him an explanation that had only made him want her even more. He'd driven home that night in a state of angry frustration, wondering grimly if the proverbial cold shower could put out the fires that raged inside him.

The loudspeaker crackled with static as each event was announced. There was trick riding and fancy roping, steer wrestling and saddle bronc riding, calf roping and the event for cutting horses.

KayCee watched excitedly as the contestants put their cutting horses through their paces. "I'll bet Teddy can do that, right, Dad?"

"Teddy's the best there is," he said proudly.

"Did you ever enter him in competition?" asked Jenna.

"I'm not big on crowds," he confessed. "And I can't imagine anyone but me working Teddy."

At the next announcement, the crowd went wild.

"They call the rodeo the suicide circuit," said Trace. "You're about to see why."

The bull riding event was one of the most exciting, because it was also one of the most perilous. Their attention was drawn to chute number three, where a rider was carefully lowering himself onto the back of a thousand pounds of bristling fury.

At the signal, the gate was opened and the brahma bull exploded from the chute. Using only one hand, the cowboy attempted to cling for the full eight-second ride, while the angry bull twisted and turned in an effort to be rid of its rider. With one furious burst to the side, it sent the cowboy to the ground with a bone-jarring thud. The bull gave chase, its horns down in an attempt to gore the hapless cowboy. The rodeo clowns sprang into action, diverting the bull by popping in and out of barrels, providing hilarious entertainment for the crowd with their life-saving antics.

KayCee's face was bright and eager as she watched the competition heat up. She leaned forward in her seat and proclaimed to Jenna, "I'll bet my dad could stay on one of those bulls!"

From everything Jenna knew and sensed about Trace McCall, she was inclined to agree, and she couldn't resist asking, "How come you aren't competing?"

Sitting beside him, she felt the heated brush of his arm against hers as he lifted his shoulders in a shrug. "I prefer my competition on a one-on-one basis, strictly between me and the animal. I have nothing to prove to anyone, least of all to thousands of screaming spectators. Besides, breaking mustangs for a living isn't much different from trying to stay on a bucking bull, only for me the ride is longer and the pay's a lot less."

Sensing a subterfuge, Jenna ventured, "And the rodeo is no place to raise a kid, right?"

He turned his head away from the action in the arena to look at her, his eyes bright with the possibility that maybe she understood after all.

What Jenna understood was that Trace was the kind of man who did what he had to do when it came to raising his daughter—from the harsh ultimatum he had issued to his ex-wife, to the grueling day-to-day existence of making a living, making sacrifices along the way, but never once compromising the fierce self-confidence that was so much a part of him.

She understood, also, the bitterness that fueled his emotions, and how important it was to him to instill in KayCee the pride of being Sioux. But how could she really understand what it was like to be an Indian, or the very real fear he had of losing custody of his daughter, when she herself had never experienced anything like it?

KayCee's voice piped up over the din of the crowd. "When's the barrel racing, Dad?"

He knew what KayCee was asking and didn't have the heart to tell her that her mother wouldn't be performing. The Sylvie he knew craved the glitter as much as any performer. If she was present, surely she would have paraded around the arena to the cheers and shouts of the crowd during the grand entry.

Hoping to find some way to tell her later, he changed the subject in a hurry. "Is anyone hungry?"

"I am!" Jenna and KayCee exclaimed in unison.

"I'll get us something to eat."

He stood up and brushed Jenna's legs with the backs of his knees as he squeezed past her toward the aisle.

Jenna drew her legs in close, but there was no avoiding the warm surge of electricity that went through her at the contact. She wondered weakly why even the barest touch from this man was like an exercise in intimacy.

She was puzzled, also, by the way Trace was acting. When he arrived at her house to pick her up that morning, she had attributed his uncharacteristic inability to make eye contact to his apprehension over the possibility of seeing Sylvie again. The rejection he had received at her own front door the other night had only added to the tension in the morning air. Once the festivities got under way, however, he had seemed to grow more relaxed. It was as if the one person he dreaded seeing most wasn't even there.

The possibility hit Jenna with the impact of a runaway train. Sylvie wasn't here, and somehow Trace knew it. That would explain his shift in mood, and why he had changed the subject when KayCee asked about the barrel-racing competition.

Jenna's gaze flew to the unsuspecting child. If only there were some way she could avert the disappointment that was in store for KayCee.

Trace returned with hot dogs and Cokes for the three of them and a huge pink cotton-candy cone for KayCee.

Jenna waited until KayCee's attention was torn between the action in the arena and the spun sugar, before turning to Trace. "She's not here, is she?"

He didn't ask her what she meant; he didn't have to. His tone echoed both his relief and his fury when he answered simply, "It doesn't look like it."

He turned away from the questions he saw written in Jenna's eyes. Yes, KayCee was bound to be disappointed, and no, damn it, he didn't know when or how he was going to tell her.

The bareback bronc riding was announced, and the matter was left unresolved as they turned their attention to the first horse that bucked wildly out into the ring. For eight seconds, the cowboy used all his strength to stay on, using only one hand to hold the grip that was attached to a strap around the horse's girth. At the sound of the buzzer, he was helped to dismount by one of the pickup men. When his score was announced, a general murmur of disagreement ran through the crowd. "Why so low?" Jenna questioned. "He stayed on, didn't he?"

"It wasn't the rider," said Trace. "It was the horse. Points are awarded for the rider's performance and for the horse's. That's why a good rider hopes to draw a difficult horse. That horse just didn't have it."

Into Jenna's mind sprang a vision of Trace, all angry grace and symmetry of motion, astride the mean-spirited buckskin, and she knew there wasn't a single rider in the competition who could rival him. He had too much skill and talent, and a natural inclination toward danger, for him to be anything other than the best, and she knew, also, that the rodeo was one of the sacrifices he had made.

"That rider shoulda been on Buck," KayCee exclaimed.

"Buck would have given him a high-scoring ride, that's for sure," Trace agreed.

"It's too bad Buck's future doesn't include the rodeo," said Jenna.

"What?" KayCee looked aghast. "You wouldn't do that, would you, Dad? You wouldn't sell Buck to the rodeo, would you?"

Jenna hadn't realized that her unwitting remark would cause such a reaction, and she spoke up quickly to avert a scene. "Of course he wouldn't. He told me himself he wanted to train Buck for cutting. Isn't that right, Trace?"

Selling Buck to the rodeo was precisely what he was thinking. Still, he wasn't lying when he forced a smile and replied, "Yes, Jenna, that's what I said."

But when KayCee's attention was riveted once again on the competition, Jenna voiced her own concern. "You wouldn't, would you?"

He dropped his voice low, so that only she could hear. "Don't be too sure about that."

"But you said—"

"I know what I said. Maybe I've changed my mind."

"What about KayCee?"

"Business is business, Jenna. I can't help it if she's formed some crazy attachment to that horse."

He reached over and grabbed KayCee's hand. "Let's go walk around for a while. I'll bet there's lots of things going on in the back."

"Okay," she said happily. "And maybe we can find out when the barrel racing will be."

Trace gave Jenna an uncertain look over his shoulder as the three of them filed out of the bleachers.

They wandered around behind the scenes, where handlers rushed around and impatient animals pawed the ground in their corrals and pens.

Trace bought a candy apple for KayCee and received a disapproving look from Jenna.

"I know," he said as he watched his daughter skip on ahead, "too much sweets. But the kid's in for a letdown, so let her have a little fun while she can."

"When do you plan on telling her?"

She had an infernal knack for getting to the heart of a matter and not letting him sidestep the issue. A pained look crossed his handsome face, and he answered impatiently, "I don't know, Jenna. I just don't know. Do you have any suggestions?"

Her own uncomfortable expression gave him his answer.

"Right," he muttered. "I didn't think so."

"Hey, look!" KayCee said jubilantly. "Ellen's here today with her mom and dad. Can I go over and visit with them for a while?"

The silent look Trace gave Jenna asked if now was the time.

She replied with a subtle shake of the head, a movement barely perceptible, except to someone watching as closely as he was.

"Sure, go on. We'll be back for you in a while." He rumpled her hair affectionately and sent her off.

"Thanks for saving me from having to tell her." He was unaccustomed to expressing gratitude—that much was evident in the grudging tone in his voice.

Those ebony eyes said so much as his intense look poured over her face. Jenna knew that look. She'd seen it the other night, just before he kissed her. Strolling by his side, his intimidating presence making itself more evident by the occasional brush of his arm against hers, she struggled to keep her voice level and calm.

"I didn't do it for you. Something tells me you can take care of yourself. I did it for KayCee. It just didn't seem like the right time. Sometimes it's best to let things run their own course."

Like this crazy feeling he stirred up inside her that made her question her own convictions. Given time, would it, too, run its course? Or would it grow stronger, devouring her logic the way his beautiful black eyes were devouring her face?

"Come on," he said. "There's something I want you to see."

He grasped her hand unexpectedly, and she could feel the scrape of his callused palm against hers as he led her into the dark spaces beneath the bleachers, and back out into the bright sunshine, to an area behind the stands, where the bulls were penned.

"Over there, see him?" He pointed to a small corral behind all the others.

Through the rails of the fencing Jenna saw a brindled bull standing in the middle of the enclosure.

They threaded their way down the narrow aisles between the corrals for a better look.

"He looks old," she said. "Is he dangerous?"

"Dangerous enough so that they don't let him compete anymore. His name's Clover, but don't let that fool you. The Sioux have a name for a bull like that. *Witko Tatanka.* Crazy bull. He's been around the circuit for years. He's gored almost every rider that's gotten on his back. I've got the scars from those horns on my leg to prove it."

Jenna turned her back on the aged bull in the corral and said, surprised, "I thought you said you don't compete."

"I don't. Not anymore. I used to, though, a little, before KayCee was born. That's how I met Sylvie. We were both trying our hand at competition. Needless to say, she's become a success."

"Giving up your child in the process is hardly the mark of a successful person," said Jenna. "Making a go of a hard situation, working from sunup until

sundown, raising a child alone and doing a good job
of it, now that's what I'd call success."

She spoke impulsively, not realizing what she'd said
until she saw the stunned look on his face.

"What I mean is…" She nibbled the corner of her
bottom lip and dropped her gaze beneath a sweep of
black lashes. With shy reluctance, she confessed, "I
don't think you're doing such a bad job of it."

It was as if she'd been caught with her hand in the
cookie jar. Trace smiled wickedly and ventured, "Is
that a compliment, teacher?"

She had tried so hard to fault him in the beginning, so certain had she been that KayCee's troubles
all sprang from his inattention. Yet the better she
knew him, the harder it became to blame him for
something she now knew was much more complicated than that.

"Maybe. Just a little one." She smiled impishly up
at him. "Not that I think you deserve it."

"No woman speaks to a Sioux warrior like that and
gets away with it." There was a hint of gentle self-
mocking in his silken purr.

She could smell the musk that came from his pores,
that healthy, clean male smell that set her pulse racing. It was deserted behind the stock pens, and curi-
ously untouched by the sounds of the crowd. The
only thing that stood between them was the summer
wind. A rising gust picked up a strand of her hair and
blew it into her lashes. She blinked to untangle it, but
it was Trace's fingers, as soft as a whisper against her
temple, that set it free.

His finger slid, without premeditation, along the side of her face to trace the contour of her cheek. "Your skin feels like the petals of a new spring flower," he murmured, "soft as velvet, smooth as glass."

She was surprised that a man as rugged as he was would be that familiar with the touch of a flower petal, but then she realized it was because he was an Indian and was in tune with the natural world in primitive and intimate ways most people were not. There was something feverishly compelling in his differentness. It told her that he was the kind of man who could protect a woman with his strength and show her things with his sensitive Indian soul that she would never have dreamed possible.

His gaze fell to her mouth and boldly lingered as he moved his thumb back and forth across the fullness of her bottom lip. For such a hard, uncompromising man, his touch was incredibly soft.

Jenna's pulse soared, and it took all her strength to keep her lips from parting.

He felt her resistance, even though she hadn't moved a muscle. "Jenna, the other night, I...I didn't mean to come on so strong. When you grow up on an Indian reservation, you learn that you don't always get what you want. Sometimes you have to take it. But I've never taken a woman against her will and I'm not about to start. If you and I make love, it'll be because we both want it, even if it is just for the night. Beyond that..."

His eyes were dark and pleading as they probed hers. "I don't know, Jenna. I didn't plan on any of this."

"That's all right, Trace," she said softly. "Neither did I."

His hands settled at her waist and drew her slowly closer. "I meant what I said the other night, about wanting you. The fact is, Jenna, I don't think I've ever wanted anyone more. So if I come on like gangbusters, just remember that old habits are hard to break."

Somehow, her hands had come to rest upon his arms, fingers gently kneading the biceps that rippled beneath his shirt. "It's not true what they say about old dogs, you know."

"Are you calling me an old dog?" On his face was the lusty smile of a man about to kiss a woman.

"And what if I am?" In her eyes was the gleam of a woman about to be kissed.

"You'll have to pay the price for that."

Jenna lowered her lashes so that he wouldn't see the eagerness in her eyes, and asked, "And what price is that?"

"I'm afraid I'm going to have to kiss you."

She peered up at him. "Right here?"

He nodded gravely. "And right now."

"I don't suppose there's anything I could do to talk you out of it."

"Just remember what I said about old habits."

She came easily into his arms. Her lips parted, tongue flicking over them to moisten them with anticipation. Her head tilted back, and she could feel the heavy brush of her hair against her neck. One strong arm wound around her waist, pulling her against the hard length of him. Her pulse soared and her eyes closed, but the kiss that every nerve ending was screaming for never came.

Jenna heard the bellow of the bull just as it slammed into the fence, but Trace was already in motion, jerking her away in the nick of time from the horns that thrashed through the railing. The impact reverberated along the entire fence and seemed to shake the very ground upon which they were standing.

She turned quickly to look over her shoulder, and what she saw sent a bolt of terror through her. The bull that had looked so old and tired only minutes ago pawed the ground with one hoof, head low, horns braced, stirring up the arid dust with each angry snort of its flaring nostrils. It was about to charge again.

Trace pulled her roughly away. They watched from a safer distance as the bull charged the fence again, splintering the oak post with its massive strength and fury.

"Damn it," Trace swore angrily. "I know how bad that old bull is. How could I have jeopardized your safety like that?"

Jenna's heart was beating frantically from the close call. "It's—it's all right," she managed between gasping breaths.

"No, it isn't," he snapped. "I should have known better." His eyes were dark and fierce and filled with self-reproach. "Let's get out of here."

His strong body radiated a powerful force as he pivoted on his bootheels and stalked away, cursing to himself over the way she made him run contrary to his own instincts.

It wasn't like him to be so out of control. Lust was one thing, but this was something else, something much more dangerous. For the hundredth time, he warned himself against falling in love with another white woman, especially one with the ability to turn his world upside down and his insides out.

They found KayCee where they'd left her, finishing off the last of her candy apple.

"The barrel racing ought to be soon, don't you think, Dad?"

He had to tell her...now. He gathered his wits about him and set himself to the difficult task. Slinging an arm around her shoulder, he pulled her close to his side and said, "Hey, kiddo, there's something I have to tell you."

She looked up at him quizzically. "Sure, Dad. What?"

Trace swallowed hard and opened his mouth to speak, hoping the right words would come. "I know you thought—"

The remainder of his words were drowned out by the static hum of the loudspeaker.

"That's it, Dad! Did you hear? The barrel racing's next!"

Why was he feeling guilty, when he had no reason to be? It wasn't his fault Sylvie wasn't there. He tried to summon up some indignation for KayCee's benefit. "It's about—"

"Listen, Dad, they're announcing the contestants!"

"KayCee, this is important. I'm trying to tell you that—"

The voice that blared from the crackling loudspeaker silenced his attempt.

"Ladies and gentlemen, the sweetheart of the rodeo..."

Trace's extremities went cold with dread.

"...Sylvie McCall!"

And then numb with shock.

The name resounded in his brain like gunfire. A lock of black hair sliced his cheek as he whipped his head around to find Jenna. His eyes met hers across the dust-filled distance.

Trace turned back to KayCee and put his hand on her shoulder. Steering her around toward the arena, he said, "We'd better get over there, if we want to get a good spot."

KayCee fidgeted as they waited for the first contestant to come out. One minute she'd been brimming with excitement. Now she hung a little closer to Jenna's side, finding an unexpected comfort there as the realization of what was about to happen suddenly caught up with her.

She spoke up to hide the nervousness that was evident nevertheless. "Were you saying something before, Dad?"

Trace feigned a sternness he did not really feel and said, "Only that if you keep eating all that junk, you're going to have a bellyache later on."

"Okay, Dad."

But he knew by the way she let his observation go unchallenged that she wasn't really listening. Her eyes, like his, were riveted on the gate.

Chapter 7

She was blond, blue-eyed and beautiful. The sunlight sparkled off her rhinestone costume as she dismounted her big yellow horse and came toward them.

Jenna was seized by a feeling strongly akin to jealousy at the thought that Trace had once loved this woman. She could feel his presence beside her. He was tense and on guard. She chanced a quick look at him. His face yielded so little, yet she knew how vulnerable he was at this moment. It only made him more attractive, for it tarnished that air of arrogance and let the human side of him show through. She wanted to take his hand and give it a reassuring squeeze, but she knew he wouldn't like that, not when it was so important for him to shore up his defenses.

She was standing before them now, this woman of

golden light and sequins, her eyes impossibly blue and fixed on KayCee.

"Hi, darlin'. Well, now, you sure are getting big."

Her voice carried a soft twang, and her sentences turned up at the end, as if she were asking questions when she wasn't.

"Come on, now, don't you have a kiss for me?"

KayCee left her place by Jenna's side and came forward to plant a tentative kiss on Sylvie's cheek.

"That's much better. I brought you a present, darlin'. It's over there in my saddlebag. Why don't you go on over and get it? Don't you worry none about Bramble," she said of the big palomino, when KayCee hesitated. "He's as gentle as can be."

"I'm not afraid of horses," KayCee said defensively.

"'Course you're not, darlin'. Maybe I'll even let you ride him later. Go on."

She turned her dazzling smile on Trace.

"It's good to see you again, Trace. You're looking good, real good. But then, you were always just about the handsomest man I've ever known."

Why was she making those eyes at him, when they both knew it didn't matter anymore? And then he realized that it was all part of the performance. She'd been smiling and twinkling those eyes at crowds for so long, she wasn't even aware when she was doing it.

"Thanks, Sylvie," he said. "You look pretty good yourself."

He was relieved that his voice sounded normal, despite the way his emotions were colliding. He stood stock-still, making no move to kiss her or even take her hand.

"That was a pretty good time you turned in." He nodded toward the palomino. "He's a beauty."

"I got him a couple of years ago in Denver, and since then I've shaved two seconds off my time. He reminds me a little of Teddy. How is that old mustang these days?"

A little pain flared inside him when he thought about Teddy getting old, but he masked it, determined to show her no weakness. "He stumbled recently, but he's all right."

He reached behind him for Jenna's hand and drew her forward. "Sylvie, this is Jenna Ward, KayCee's teacher at the elementary school. Jenna, this is KayCee's mom."

Jenna was glad he hadn't introduced Sylvie to her as his ex-wife, for that would have added an intimacy that she had begun to think of as hers. She extended her hand and said, "That was some magnificent riding."

"Why, thank you, darlin'. The first round's behind me, with a good score. I think I can take this competition. What do you think, Trace?"

He replied stoically, "I think you can do anything you set your mind to, Sylvie."

"Dad, look." KayCee returned and held up a smaller version of the sparkling shirt Sylvie was wearing.

"It's beautiful," said Jenna.

"I can wear it when I ride Buck."

"Buck?" Sylvie questioned. "What happened to Sweetbriar? Did you get KayCee a new horse, Trace?"

Trace shot an irritated look at KayCee. "No, I didn't get KayCee a new horse. She still rides Sweetbriar."

He was spared the necessity of having to explain about Buck when several people approached them.

Sylvie's blue eyes sparkled as brightly as the sequins on her cowgirl outfit as she acquiesced to their requests for an autograph. For several minutes she chatted amiably with them.

Jenna was caught off guard by Sylvie McCall. She'd come today expecting to meet a hard, driven woman who was more in love with the glitter of the rodeo than with her own husband. Instead, she'd met a smiling, gregarious woman who had simply made some different choices from the ones she herself would have made. It came down to priorities, she supposed, and Sylvie's were obviously elsewhere.

With a shock, Jenna realized that KayCee was nothing more to Sylvie than a fan. Not quite as adoring as most, however, judging from KayCee's aloofness. Despite the glittering gift, KayCee was maintaining her distance. What, after all, was a twelve-year-old to make of it all?

When Sylvie was finished signing autographs, Trace said to Jenna in a low voice, "I'll be right back. Keep her here with you." He gestured toward KayCee, who was preoccupied with her present, holding it this way and that to make the rhinestones glitter in the sunlight. Jenna nodded and sent him off with a reassuring smile. She watched as he made his way over to Sylvie.

Standing off to the side, Jenna noticed that neither of them was smiling. KayCee was watching, too. What thoughts, she wondered, were running through KayCee's mind at the obviously strained reunion of her parents? Moments later she was taken aback when the girl turned her face up at her and asked guilelessly, "Do you think my dad's handsome?"

Caught off balance by the question, Jenna stammered, "I think . . . I think . . ." She glanced over to where Trace stood, face impassive, stance combative, looking indescribably attractive. She felt powerless against the impact, and said helplessly, "I think your father's very handsome."

"Yeah, me too. I look a lot like him."

She looked back down at KayCee and smiled at the pride in her tone. Personally, she was glad it was Trace's beautiful black eyes, and not Sylvie's shimmering blue ones, that she looked into whenever she looked at KayCee. She could not help but wonder what impact the absence of any of Sylvie's physical characteristics had on KayCee. She could remember looking in the mirror when she was little and seeing exactly the opposite—a face that looked nothing like her father's, but resembled instead the one she saw for two weeks each summer and on holidays.

"You sure do," she said. She slung an arm around KayCee's shoulder and felt no resistance. Another time, another place, and she would have confided to KayCee how very much alike they were. But with the crowd pressing in all around them, it would have to wait. Her gaze shifted again to Trace and Sylvie. Again there came that feeling inside, like scores of tiny lances jabbing at her, arousing in her something she could only define as jealousy. What were those two talking about over there that had Trace trying so hard to look unaffected, when she knew otherwise?

"You're in your element, Sylvie, that's for sure."

Trace's face was drawn in a serious expression. His voice was businesslike, in spite of the compliment. It was important to maintain his distance, and even more important to impart the impression that he was doing just fine.

"I can't deny I love it," she replied.

His gaze tightened on her face. "More than anything?"

She knew from the dangerously low tone of his voice where this was heading. "Trace, darlin', let's not get into that and spoil this beautiful day, okay?"

"Why not, Sylvie? Think it'll ruin your next ride?"

"It was never in your nature to be cruel, Trace."

"Maybe. But I notice you haven't answered the question."

"No, I don't think it will ruin my next ride."

"Not that question, Sylvie. I asked you if you love competing more than anything."

"What do you want me to say?" she complained petulantly. "That I love it more than I love you? I told you five years ago that—"

"More than you love *me?*" he echoed, his voice thinning with astonishment. "You think this is about me?" He laughed abruptly. It was a sound born more of cold fury than of irony. "I know you'd like to think I've been obsessing over you these past five years, but the fact is, Sylvie, I've managed to put my life back together and get on with it. I was talking about your daughter. KayCee. Remember her?''

"I love KayCee," she asserted. "You know I do." Those blue eyes looked at him pleadingly from beneath the brim of her white Stetson, imploring him not to refute what she'd said.

It would have been so easy to hurt her. For several moments, he agonized over whether or not to tell her what a rotten mother she was, but she looked scared and defenseless in the shadow of his mounting anger, and the words wouldn't come.

He shifted restlessly from foot to foot and demanded, "So, what are your plans? Are you staying, or what?''

"Staying? Well, no, darlin'. There's the Wyoming State Fair in Douglas the first week in August, and I'm registered for Frontier Days in Riverton after that, and— What? Why are you looking at me like that? You know I can't stay."

"What about KayCee?"

"I might be able to make it back for a couple of days after Riverton. If not, I'll see her here in Crandall next year." She saw his face harden like steel and said defensively, "Why do you think I even compete here each year? The prize money's certainly nothing to speak of. I could easily be competing in Cheyenne for big money, but I'm not. I know what you think of me, Trace, and you've got every right to think it, but I love KayCee, and that's why I come back to this nothing little place every year."

He knew then that his fears were unfounded. Nothing had changed. She didn't want custody of KayCee now any more than she had the day she walked out. He didn't know whether to hug her or hate her for it.

"We all have to make our sacrifices, I guess."

She accepted his sarcasm as penalty for her guilt. She saw him smile, yet failed to notice that it didn't reach his eyes. "You know," she said, testing his reaction to each word as it left her mouth, "it's going to be hard for me to get out to the house."

"Hey, no problem." What problem could there be, Trace thought contemptuously, except that KayCee just might be devastated that she didn't have the time to stop by?

"Are you going to stick around for the closing ceremonies? They're going to crown the rodeo queen."

"We'll see." But Trace already knew they'd be long gone before that spectacle.

Sylvie knew it, too. "Will I at least see you and KayCee after the next round?"

In spite of all the contempt and the bitterness and the anger, Trace didn't have the heart to say no. KayCee was, after all, Sylvie's daughter, too. "Sure, Sylvie. We'll see you again later."

She flashed him one of those smiles that made the crowd go wild. "Wish me luck?"

These last few years, Trace had wondered what lingering effect she would have on him. But as he looked into those blue eyes, sheltered from the blistering sunshine by the brim of her hat, he felt himself oddly impervious to her appeal. Her eyes were blue and bright, but they lacked the depth of emotion he saw in Jenna's eyes. Her prettiness failed to move him to breathlessness, the way Jenna's natural beauty did. His fingers remained motionless at his sides, unaffected by the sight of her golden hair, instead of twitching involuntarily with the impulse they invariably had to tangle themselves in the rich, dark fullness of Jenna's.

The realization that she posed no threat to his custody of KayCee or his desire enabled Trace to smile at her. This time the smile was genuine, softening his features to near perfection and crinkling the corners of his eyes to make them glitter like jet in the warm July sunshine. He gave her a thumbs-up and turned and walked away.

"I told your mom we'd see her later," he told KayCee when he rejoined them. "Is that okay with you?"

KayCee offered a haphazard shrug, but from the easy way her hand slid into Jenna's, Trace knew the encounter with Sylvie hadn't been easy for her. He was seized by an impulse to take his daughter by the shoulders and shake her and ask what she'd expected—that her mother would want to be a part of her life? Hurt me, he railed silently against Sylvie. Hurt me all you want, but don't hurt KayCee. Yet he knew that, for all his strength, he could not protect her from the pain she must be feeling.

He realized suddenly that, were it not for Jenna's presence, things could have gone a lot worse. He was grateful for the stabilizing effect she had on KayCee, and for that caring nature of hers that helped ease the sting of Sylvie's absence. And maybe, just maybe, her presence there today had helped him, too. Confronting Sylvie had somehow not been as difficult as he thought it would be, just because he'd known that Jenna was somewhere close by, rooting for him.

He was feeling relieved and triumphant and a little bit leery of these new feelings for Jenna that were just now emerging from the dust of his confrontation with Sylvie.

"Why don't you two go back to your seats? You'll be able to see the arena better from there."

"Aren't you coming with us, Dad?"

"There's something I have to do. I'll be along in a little while."

"But Mom's gonna compete again."

"I'll be back in plenty of time," he assured her. Before she could voice another objection, he disappeared into the crowd.

Hand in hand, Jenna and KayCee walked back to the stands. When they were halfway there, the static blare of the loudspeaker announced a change in the order of competition in the barrel races.

"Mom's up first!" KayCee cried. "I'd better go tell Dad."

"I'm sure he heard—"

The words weren't even out of Jenna's mouth before KayCee pulled her hand away and darted off.

With a cry, Jenna ran after her. "KayCee! Come back!"

KayCee zigzagged her way through the crowd, stopping now and then to stand on tiptoe, trying to spot her father. She couldn't find him anywhere.

Then she remembered the direction he and Jenna had taken earlier.

It was cool and dark and spooky beneath the bleachers. Her eyes darted left and right, searching the shadows for goblins and monsters as she hurried along. When she was out in the sunshine again, her black braids glistened and whipped around as she turned her head in all directions, looking for him. Her heart sank. She was about to turn back when she heard voices streaming through the open door of one of the trailers.

"Your price is mighty high, Trace," she heard a man's voice say.

"Maybe, Bill," her father answered, "but he's just about the best I've seen. I tell you, I haven't had one like him in a long time."

"And he sent you to the ground every time?"

"Every time."

"Hell, Trace, I've seen you ride, and any horse that can throw you has got to be worth the price. You've got a deal."

"Congratulations, Bill. You've got yourself one mean buckskin mustang. I'll bring him by next week."

KayCee stood out of sight, listening, the blood draining from her face. It couldn't be. He'd said he wouldn't do it. Jenna had said he wouldn't do it. Yet she'd just overheard her father sell Buck to the rodeo. Devastated, she turned and walked numbly away.

Jenna spotted KayCee emerging from beneath the bleachers and ran to her. "You scared me half to

death, running off like that." But when she saw the
glum look on KayCee's face, she couldn't be angry
with her. "Did you find him?"

"No," she lied.

"KayCee, what's wrong?"

"Nothin'," the girl replied unconvincingly.

Misinterpreting, Jenna said, "Don't worry, he said
he'd be back before your mother's next round."

He'd also said he wouldn't sell Buck to the rodeo,
yet he was doing it. KayCee was devastated in the face
of such logic—and just when she'd really begun to
make some headway with the mustang. Putting on a
brave face, she said, "We'd better go back now, or
we'll miss Mom."

The rest of the afternoon passed in a blur. Trace
returned to his seat just in time to see Sylvie put her
spurs to the big palomino and cut those cloverleaf
patterns in record-breaking time. For KayCee's benefit, he clapped as loudly as everyone else, and even
whistled shrilly through his teeth to show there were
no hard feelings.

Afterward, they traipsed back down to meet Sylvie behind the scenes and said their awkward good-
byes before Sylvie got swallowed up by a ring of
adoring fans.

On the ride home, KayCee sat between Trace and
Jenna in the front seat of Trace's pickup, looking as
if her world were coming to an end.

Jenna tried without success to coax her out of her
sullen mood. "I'd never been to a rodeo before. I
want to thank you both for inviting me along." Her
effort was met with acute silence. She cast a worried

look over at Trace. He drove with his eyes fixed on the road, a hard, resolute I-told-you-so expression stamped on his handsome face.

He'd known this would happen. Why had he let Jenna talk him into letting KayCee go to that damned rodeo? He had learned to deal with the blows that life dealt, but KayCee was just a kid. His heart ached for her, and if there was any way he could have taken her pain onto his own shoulders, he would have gladly done it, to keep her from having to grow up too soon.

He saw the tears well in her eyes. Reaching around her with his right arm, he pulled her protectively to him. Seeking to dry the tears he thought were caused by her mother's rejection, he spoke to her in their native language, softly, soothingly, lovingly, telling her things that were meant only for her.

KayCee's tears slowly subsided. She loved her father, in spite of his betrayal, and felt safe in his strong embrace. But there was no sense taking any chances. As she snuggled against his side, listening to his softly crooning voice, her mind was feverishly at work on a way to set Buck free.

Chapter 8

The barn was dark and cool, even in the heat of midday. The pungent aroma of hay and horseflesh permeated the air, drifting upward to irrevocably scent the knotted beams of the pitched roof.

A shaft of sunlight sliced the dim interior from a window high in the loft, its myriad particles of dust dancing like diamonds all through it. It fell upon naked shoulders, glancing off the soft sheen of perspiration that covered them, making the dark skin glisten.

Trace held the upturned hoof of one of the horses wedged between his knees. His back broadened, the lean muscles flexing as he hunched over it. Ribbons of black hair spilled unchecked down the sides of his face, but he made no attempt to brush them back.

It took only moments and a seasoned hand to pry the culprit loose with the pocketknife he carried in the back pocket of his jeans. It was a small pebble, but big enough to make the horse lame if allowed to stay lodged beneath its shoe for too long. Just like some problems, Trace thought wryly as he walked the horse through the scattered hay back to its stall. Enough to drive a man crazy.

He'd spent all last night with his back pressed against the trunk of a tree, staring at the stars in the midnight sky, trying to sort it all out, just as he had done dozens of other times. Only last night had been different. With the coming of dawn, something had changed. It had been imperceptible at first. Someone without his acute Indian senses might not even have been aware of it. But he'd learned at an early age to be aware of things around him and within him, to count himself a part of it all in some way that was never really a conscious thought at all, just something that came naturally, like breathing.

The old feelings of anger and bitterness were still there, but a new feeling had grown within him. Like the dawn, its first faint traces of light touching the tops of the trees, it emerged gradually, until it came upon him like the blinding light of day, chasing away the shadows and bringing everything into sharp focus.

Last night he had come to grips with the awful gnawing in the pit of his stomach caused by his need for Jenna Ward. It was more than lust, and that was what scared him. It left him open and aching and still feeling the aftershocks as he went through the motions of removing the horse's bridle. He closed the door to the stall and turned to leave.

A figure stood at the open door to the barn, tall and slender, silhouetted against the white sunlight from outside.

He'd know those slim hips and long legs anywhere. The effect on him was always the same. It began with a constriction in his throat and moved slowly downward to flood his loins with heat. She came forward, passing from light into shadow and driving him crazy with the long, slow, unrehearsed seduction of her strides. He stood there, unable to say or do anything, the bridle dangling from his hand.

"Hello, Trace."

His eyes, accustomed to the darkness inside the barn, took in all of her at once, the stone-washed jeans hugging her hips, the roundness of her breasts pressing against the fabric of her blue chambray shirt, her dark hair loose and brushing her shoulders like a great shaggy mane.

Get hold of yourself, man, he told himself. It's only your hormones working overtime. Then he remembered last night and the realization of his need for her, and he knew that anything he was telling himself now was a lie.

It was just his cursed luck, feeling this way about another Anglo woman. Accepting the powerful effect she had on him with a mixture of anger and resignation, he hung the bridle on a peg outside the stall and came forward. "Hi, Jenna. What brings you here today?" It wasn't her he was angry at, it was himself, for the easy way he'd let her slip past his defenses. It shone in his eyes, despite the softly eager tone of his voice.

He looked so primal and beautiful that it literally stole Jenna's breath away. But what did she expect? He was in his element here among the mustangs, his body one moment glistening in a ray of sunshine as if he'd rubbed it with bear grease, the next enveloped in shadow like a phantom, ebony eyes gleaming at her through the shadows.

One word came to mind to describe him, hitting Jenna with the impact of a Mack truck.

Indian.

It was what he was. It was who he was. It was a potent combination of wildness and sensitivity that made him different from anyone she'd ever known. In his eyes she saw the age-old hostility of the Sioux staring back at her, and in spite of the pleasant greeting, there was nothing friendly about him.

"I came to see how KayCee's feeling."

In the next instant, whatever had put that look in his eyes disappeared as he shook his head and said, "That was some bellyache she had Sunday night. Hell, she ate everything in sight at that damned rodeo. But except for the silent treatment she's been giving me all week, she seems fine." Even now, several days later, Trace was still reproaching himself for taking KayCee to Crandall. She'd cried herself to sleep that night, just like she'd done the time before, and having a bellyache hadn't helped matters any. He'd taken a little dried pulverized root of the cattail flag and steeped it in hot water with the white base of the leaves, the way his mother had shown him how to do a long time ago, and given the warm drink to KayCee. His own head had been pounding, so he'd swallowed a cold infusion of what his people called the blue medicine to relieve the ache.

"Then why didn't she show up at school today? Really, Trace, just because it was a half day, that didn't mean you could just keep her home."

"Whoa! Back up a bit! What do you mean, she didn't show up at school today? I drove her to the bus stop myself this morning, like I always do. Great! Don't tell me now she's cutting school. She's probably up at the house, back in bed, watching one of those crazy game shows, pretending to be sick."

He felt a growing desperation to believe that what he'd just said was true, but he knew it wasn't like KayCee to feign illness. For what? To stay home from school? She never asked to stay home. For all her complaining about Billy Hobbs, she appeared to genuinely like school. Trace knew that Jenna had a lot to do with that. Yet for all Jenna had come to mean to him, there was nothing she could do to prevent the panic from welling up inside of him. He shoved past her and half walked, half ran to the door.

Outside, in the bright sunshine, Trace scoured the area for a sign, a clue, something that would tell him what he wanted to know. And then he saw it.

There on the dusty ground, his Indian eyes picked out two sets of hoofprints among all the others scattered about. They were heading away from the ranch in a westerly direction. One set of hooves was shod, the other unshod. A cold, uncertain dread came over him. He backed away from the hoofprints, eyes widening with realization, then spun quickly around and dashed back toward the barn.

He raced right past Jenna, who had followed him outside and was watching with a look of growing concern. His heart pounded. His brain pleaded, *"Don't let it be."*

He rounded the corner of the barn and stopped dead in his tracks. Up ahead, the small corral where he'd put the buckskin mustang earlier was empty. A quick glance toward the south pasture, where he'd turned Sweetbriar out that morning, confirmed his fears.

Jenna watched dumbfounded as he sprinted toward the house. With inexplicable panic, she ran after him.

He took the porch steps in one long stride and yanked open the screen door. She thought for a moment that he was on his way upstairs to confirm that KayCee was curled up in bed, watching television, yet there was something awful about the fear she saw in his eyes that told her not to expect it. He wasn't in the house long enough to go upstairs. Moments later, he emerged with his rifle in his hand, and Jenna knew what she'd suspected in her heart all along. Something was terribly wrong.

"What is it? What are you doing?" She had to run to keep up with his long powerful strides.

"She's done it," he said, breathless with anger and worry. "She's taken the buckskin."

"What do you mean, she's taken him? For what?"

"How the hell should I know? Probably to set him free."

The aroma of horses and stale hay rushed into her nostrils when she followed Trace back into the barn. Her eyes making a rapid adjustment to the darkness, she watched as he pulled a saddle down from the door of an empty stall and carried it over to Teddy.

The horse sensed that something was wrong. Its ears were pricked forward and the hairs along its back bristled as the saddle blanket was thrown on first, then the heavy tooled saddle.

With practiced motions, Trace reached under the horse for the cinch. In less time than it took to think about it, Teddy was saddled and ready.

"I'm going with you," Jenna announced.

Trace thrust a boot into the stirrup and rose into the air, landing astride the sorrel's back as if he'd sprouted wings. "Like hell you are." With a quick jab of his heels, he had Teddy at a full gallop by the time they reached the barn door.

Jenna glanced around the barn and spotted the bay mare she'd ridden the day Trace kissed her out on the prairie. Within minutes, she was saddled and galloping hard after Trace, following the dust cloud made by Teddy's flying hooves.

A lone figure sat on horseback atop a high ridge, surveying the countryside with bright, piercing eyes. This was his home, his sanctuary, and he knew it the way most people knew their own names. It was his land, belonging to him in a way that was more a unification than a possession. It was a part of him and he was a part of it, and the two were inseparable. Whoever heard of owning the land, anyway? The earth wasn't a trinket or a thing to possess. Despite the nineteenth-century logic that said you could buy a piece of land, surround it with fences and call it your own, deep in his Indian soul he knew that it was the earth who possessed all men, not the other way around.

How many times had he come to this place that overlooked the sprawling panorama below, to gaze and to wonder, but never to question. The grasses grew, the rivers flowed. Who was he to question who he was? Wasn't it enough just to be?

He gazed up at the sky and felt a sense of restlessness in the deep blue that stretched to the far horizon. Dropping the reins, he raised his arms and lifted his hands skyward. A hundred years ago he would have called to Wakan Tanka, the Great Spirit, for the power to guide him. But this was today, and he was just a father desperate to find his daughter, and besides, he wasn't sure what he believed in anymore.

He dropped his hands and picked up the reins and was about to turn his horse's head away when there came a reverberation deep within the earth. The leather creaked when he turned in the saddle to look over his shoulder. A horse and rider were galloping full tilt in his direction.

Clots of green earth flew into the air when the bay mare pulled up sharply beside him.

"Damn it, Jenna. This is between me and KayCee."

She was out of breath, her face flushed. "I know it is," she said. "But please, Trace—I'm worried about her too."

It was there in her eyes, as green as the grass in the valley below, the same fear that consumed him.

"I'm telling you, Jenna, don't try to stop me from doing what I have to do."

Her gaze shifted to the rifle tied to the back of his saddle with leather thongs. "I won't, I promise. Just let me come along."

"And if I don't?"

Her gaze stuck bravely to his. "I'll follow you anyway."

He rolled his beautiful black eyes and expelled a breath of impatience. Didn't she ever just take no for an answer? But secretly he was glad she didn't, for if she had taken no for an answer that very first day, he would never have seen her again.

"Their tracks lead down there."

Jenna followed his stony gaze out over the panorama. It was a high, dry, windy place, hard country in which to live, yet stirring in its primitive beauty. The grass was still green and thick in the valley below, not the dry brown patch it would later become as summer progressed and the sun scorched the land with its arid heat. Beyond that stretched the prairie, an ocean of softly swaying grass as high as one's knees for as far as the eye could see. Stands of sweet-scented pines bordered the ridges. Clustered in the lowlands were cottonwoods, box elders, poplars, juniper and willows. Coyotes prowled the ravines and antelope bounded through the breaks.

The summer heat shimmered above the ground in illusory undulations, playing tricks on the eyes. Jenna blinked, half imagining that she could make out the conical shapes of Lakota lodges pitched all up and down the valley, darkening the land with their numbers as the buffalo had once done.

She looked at the man sitting tall and ramrod-straight on the horse beside her. His black hair flicked about in the summer wind, unencumbered by the red bandanna he sometimes wore to keep it from his eyes. In his haste, he hadn't bothered to put on a shirt. The sunlight glanced off the lean muscles of his shoulders and across his smooth-skinned chest. He looked as wild as the land around them, and as she had the first day she'd met him, she thought of a time that no longer existed except in colorful pictographs on buffalo robes.

She could picture eagle feathers laced in his hair, dancing wildly in the wind. She could visualize a zigzag streak of lightning painted on his face, infusing those deadly good looks with a flash of recklessness. She could almost smell the musty leather of a war shield on his arm. Something flared inside her heart, startling her with the enormity of its impact. She blinked hard to shake the image, and when she looked again, the fearsome trappings were gone, and all she saw was the worried look of a father in search of his daughter.

With a subtle tensing of his knees Trace guided the sorrel down out of the hills, with Jenna and the bay mare following close behind.

They rode slowly through the valley, following the bank of a stream, where the earth was softly yielding beneath their horses' hooves. He lost the tracks in the water and cursed softly to himself in that language

Jenna didn't understand as their horses splashed through the water. His dark eyes prowled the bank searching for the place where KayCee had brought her horse out of the water.

Hours passed. The stream eventually emptied into the river that flowed from on high, moving inexorably westward, as all the rivers did, seeking the great ocean beyond, just as he was seeking something. Every instinct he had told him she had to have come this way, and if there weren't any visible tracks for him to follow, there were other signs.

No birds flew overhead, a sure indication that something, or someone, had recently passed this way. It could have been a coyote, he reasoned. Or a horse and rider. Or two horses and a rider.

Damn that miserable mustang, Trace railed to himself. There was no telling what a mean-tempered animal like that would do. His rancor mounted against the horse. With his rifle tied to the saddle behind him, he was determined to end his battle with the buckskin once and for all.

A surge of triumph went through him when he spotted the tracks up ahead, one pair shod, the other not, proceeding at a leisurely pace toward a rise in the distance. He urged his horse into a canter.

At the top of the rise, they dismounted and tethered the horses to a low-growing bush.

Trace removed his rifle from behind the saddle. In a low growl that warned Jenna not to argue, he said, "Remember now, leave this to me. And be quiet."

If the buckskin was there, he didn't want to scare him away. He wanted to get his daughter and that blasted horse and get home before dark. Tomorrow he'd put the buckskin in the trailer and drive him over to Crandall, but not before he grounded KayCee for a month for this latest stunt. And nothing Jenna could do or say was going to talk him out of it this time.

The land fell away abruptly, exposing an ugly little ravine below that was filled with scrub brush and tangled briars. His eyes fell immediately upon the buckskin mustang, pawing furiously at the ground, ears flattened against its head in a sign of danger.

"There you are, you miserable son of a—"

Another sight silenced his epithet. It was KayCee, laying inert and crumpled several yards away on the ground.

Trace's blood went cold. He didn't hear Jenna's muffled cry. In a flash, the rifle was at his shoulder, his finger on the trigger. He brought the sight to his eye and squinted into it, fixing the buckskin in the cross hairs.

He felt Jenna tugging at his arm.

"Stop, Trace! No!"

What was wrong with her? He had to kill that horse before it killed KayCee! He shook her off like rainwater and brought the rifle back to his shoulder, but she came at him again, like some crazy person.

"Trace, no! Look!"

He saw it before the words were even out of her mouth, from the corner of his eye through the sight, a blur of tawny color moving through the brush.

Before Trace could shift his aim and fire, the cougar sprinted forward to pounce on KayCee's lifeless body.

It happened fast, yet every second seemed to pass in slow motion, an agonizing eternity to Trace, who could only watch helplessly from the distance before he could raise the rifle again. In that moment, when his worst nightmare was about to come true, there came a wild cry from the ravine, like that of a wounded animal, high-pitched and frenzied. In a thunder of hooves, the mustang came rushing forward. It reared, thrashing the air with razor-sharp hooves that it brought down upon the cougar without mercy.

In seconds, it was over, and the cougar lay dead on the ground.

KayCee opened her eyes to the blurred image of her father hovering over her with a worried look on his face. Jenna was beside him, looking pale and concerned. She was too frightened to feel any fear of reprisal from either of them, too desperately happy to see them both to think of consequences.

"Oh, Daddy, I was so scared!" Her arms came up to lock around his neck. She wasn't even aware of the tears that were streaming down her cheeks as he picked her up and carried her back up the hill.

He put her down gently on the soft ground and knelt beside her. With his thumb he wiped the wetness from her face. "How could you do it, KayCee? How could you scare me like that?" His voice emerged like a ragged whisper, filled with anger and relief and scores of other emotions she could not guess at.

She looked to Jenna for support, but realized she was outnumbered when she saw the expression on Jenna's face, silently echoing her father's question.

Her young face was troubled with guilt. Between sniffles she said, "I'm sorry, Dad. I'm sorry I did it. I know you have every right to punish me for this. But please, Dad, please don't sell Buck to the rodeo!"

"What?" His black eyes narrowed suspiciously on his daughter's face. "How did you know that?"

She plucked absently at some blades of grass by her leg and bit the corner of her bottom lip. "I heard you talking to the rodeo manager."

He heard Jenna's gasp beside him and smelled the sweet fragrance of her hair rushing by when she whirled her head to look at him.

"Trace! You said you wouldn't sell Buck to the rodeo."

"No," he answered sharply. "*You* said I wouldn't sell Buck to the rodeo." He tore his angry gaze from hers and focused it back on KayCee.

"I made a deal and I intend to keep it. Would you have me go back on my word?"

"No, but—"

"I thought he might make a good cutter, but I was wrong. What else can I do with him? Don't you see, KayCee? I have no choice."

"But you do, Dad. You do. You could always set him free."

His back stiffened. "Not on your life. These horses are our bread and butter. I'm not in this business to turn them loose, KayCee."

"Then you could give him to me." She knew it was the wrong thing to say when her father's eyes flared wide with disbelief, then brightened with fury.

"Not on your life! That horse is much too dangerous for you."

"But he's not, Dad. We're friends. He likes me. He saved me from that cougar, didn't he?"

Most horses would have fled from the cougar, but not that one. He was too feisty, too ill-tempered, to turn tail. Still, Trace wasn't convinced that the buckskin had actually meant to save KayCee from the cougar. He told himself the horse had reacted to the danger of a predator, just as it would have done at any other time.

Yet there had been no signs of ill temper in the tracks he had followed. On the contrary, the unshod prints of the buckskin had moved at an easy, relaxed pace beside the shod hooves of KayCee's mount.

"Where's Sweetbriar?" Jenna asked, looking around and seeing no sign of the animal.

"He musta caught the cougar's scent," said KayCee. "He threw me and ran off."

Trace heaved a heavy sigh of frustration. "Don't worry about him. He'll find his way home. If I were you, young lady, I'd be worrying about what I'm going to do to you for this."

KayCee's chin jutted out defiantly in a gesture that reminded Jenna all too well of Trace. "Go on, punish me. I don't care."

"You can take that attitude and—"

"Trace, wait." Jenna's voice at his side, the gentle touch of her hand on his arm, stanched his own defiant response.

How very much alike they were, thought Jenna. Each stubborn to a fault and proud beyond belief. She questioned Trace with her eyes. For some seconds he said nothing, and she knew he was battling with himself over whether or not to let her interfere despite her promise that she wouldn't. How could she stand by and say nothing, when the incident was driving a wedge between Trace and KayCee that might never heal? She saw a momentary softening of his eyes, followed by a stiff, brief nod.

"KayCee," she said softly, "what makes you think that you and Buck are such good friends? I know he saved you, but honey, he could have just been scared. Horses are like that, you know."

"I know that," the girl replied with some reluctance. "But he lets me pet him and feed him."

"And what have you been feeding him?"

"Carrots, sugar cubes." She looked away guiltily. "Apples. He really likes those."

"I guess that explains why there haven't been any carrots in the stew lately," said Trace.

KayCee shrugged, grateful her father had chosen the carrots to question and not the apples.

"There's something I don't understand," said Jenna. "If you wanted to free Buck, why didn't you just open the gate and let him out?"

"Because my dad would have gone after him. I had to make sure he got far enough away so that no one would find him. That's no life for a horse, in a rodeo, with all those men on him all the time. Buck can be trained, Dad, I know he can."

She began to cry, the big salty tears that rolled down her cheeks wreaking havoc on Trace's emotions. He rolled his eyes and looked away. When he looked back, he found KayCee's and Jenna's eyes upon him, both silently pleading.

"Now wait a minute," he complained, "that's not fair."

"To whom?" Jenna demanded. "To you, or to her? Don't you think you're being just a little selfish, Trace?"

Now he'd heard everything. He jumped to his feet and began to pace angrily, back and forth, back and forth, bootheels tramping the grass in neat furrows beneath his feet. KayCee's tears were one thing, but Jenna taking her side was more than he'd bargained for.

"What do you know about making a living on the reservation?" he angrily shot at her as he paced. "If things get too difficult for you here, all you have to do is pack your bags and leave. But I can't do that. My life is here. I've experienced life off the reservation, and I don't like it. I made a choice to live here and raise my daughter here, but that doesn't mean it's easy. I have to make a living. You know that, damn it. I told you before, that horse means income to me."

"Then train him," she said.

He watched her turn back to a tearful KayCee and wind her arms around her. It wasn't so much the simple gesture that shook Trace hard. Jenna had proved herself to be a warm and caring person in spite of her outspoken nature. It was the way KayCee responded, moving easily into the arms that folded around her. It was the way she laid her head upon Jenna's breast and spilled warm tears into the fabric of her shirt. It was the recognition of the impact Jenna had, not only on KayCee's life, but on his own, as well.

Suddenly, an overwhelming sense of loneliness filled him, pointing out the void that had existed between him and Sylvie that their reunion only confirmed. He had never been in love with Sylvie. If she hadn't been expecting KayCee, they never would have gotten married. The truth was, he'd never really been in love at all.

Surely this feeling he had as he watched Jenna—this hard, driving fist smack in the middle of his solar plexus that took his breath away—surely this wasn't love. Or was it? How could he be sure, when he had never felt anything like it before?

He approached silently and stood over them a few moments more, watching them. KayCee's tears tugged at his heartstrings. Jenna's impact was more primal.

"All right," he said reluctantly. "I won't sell Buck to the rodeo."

KayCee looked up at him with tear-shiny eyes. "But you told the man at the rodeo—"

"I'll take care of that. Bill's a good man. He'll understand."

"And you'll set Buck free?" KayCee's small, tentative voice ventured.

He gave her a heated look. "Don't press your luck, KayCee."

He strode to where his horse was waiting and removed a coil of rope from the saddle horn. "How'd you get that rope around his neck?" he asked as he came forward, fashioning a lasso.

KayCee shrugged. "I don't know. He just let me."

Another fluke, Trace thought to himself as he made his way back down into the ravine.

Chapter 9

It was late afternoon, and the crowds were enormous.

Hundreds of families were camped around the dance circle, creating a scene reminiscent of the great encampments of the nineteenth century. As many as five hundred costumed male dancers were in the arena, with hundreds of women and girls joining in. For four days and nights, the people danced and feasted like in the old days, drawing a crowd of on-lookers including tourists, visitors, interested government employees and a handful of anthropologists who journeyed to the Santee Sioux Reservation each August to observe the sun dance.

In a small arbor secluded from the crowds, a handful of men danced trancelike around a tall pole that was staked in the ground, their bared chests pierced with skewers that were attached by long thongs to the pole. Around and around they danced, hour upon hour, until the thongs tore loose from their flesh.

Trace took no part in the skin piercing, watching instead in solemn silence from the perimeter. He respected the patient courage of the dancers, but felt no particular need himself for such dramatic expressions of fortitude to show his devotion to a greater power. He needed no scars upon his breast to prove his courage.

It wasn't a lack of devotion or courage that led him to turn away from the spectacle in the arbor and seek the purification of the sweat bath. It was his desperate desire for Jenna Ward, a desire that bordered dangerously on love.

The water was already boiling as he stripped himself of his shirt and jeans and underwear and bent to enter the lodge. The hot stones sizzled when he poured a dipperful of water over them. Within minutes the small, dome-shaped lodge was filled with a hot, vapory mist. The air was sweet with the fragrance of the spray of sage he used to cover himself.

He sat alone and cross-legged in the darkened lodge, his nakedness obscured in the steam that rose from the stones, recalling with bitterness the time he'd taken Sylvie to the sun dance. He couldn't bear it if he saw the same thing in Jenna's eyes, yet even as he thought it, he knew he never would. There was too much compassion and understanding in those sea-green depths. There were too many unspoken emotions that frighteningly mirrored his own.

It was all he could do to keep from admitting to himself that he had come to crave the very thought of her. Even the sound of her laughter was unforgettable, as vibrant as she was.

She wanted him, too, as much as he wanted her. She was far too ingenuous to hide it effectively. Yet something was stopping her, too, from giving in to the exquisite torment. He recalled what she had told him the night they stood outside her front door, about not being the kind of woman who did things halfway. He knew what she wanted. She wanted forever. Hell, who didn't? In some crazy way, it was even easy for him to imagine forever with a woman like Jenna.

He had wanted her so badly that night that he thought he would burst from the pressure of it. At that moment, he'd been willing to put his own fears on hold just to have her, but she hadn't been willing to do the same. How ironic, he thought, that she should hold so steadfastly to her resistance, when everything he saw in her eyes screamed surrender.

It was said that a man who failed to cleanse himself in the sweat bath would see the face of his tormenter always before him. He sat there for a long time, breathing the moist, scented air into his lungs, thinking about her, knowing that it was her face he would be carrying into his dreams for a very long time to come.

The steam of the sweat bath purified Trace's body, but it could not purge him of his desperate longing. When he emerged at last, his hair hanging straight and wet to his shoulders, the sun had disappeared behind the western peaks, tinting the evening sky with massive brush strokes of pink and violet. Ceremonial fires burned bright, sending orange pitches of flame deep into the night. The echo of the drums could be heard far out onto the prairie, the ever-steady, far-reaching heartbeat of the people.

He went to the lodge his mother had erected at the far end of the crescent. Each year he offered to help her with the poles and the canvas, and each year she refused, shooing him away as if he were a pesky horsefly and telling him it was a woman's place to erect the lodge. He swept the flap aside and bent low to enter. He wasn't surprised to find it empty. The sun dance was always an opportunity to visit friends and relatives long into the night, and he knew his mother and daughter would not be back until late.

He stripped out of his clothes again. From a stiff leather parfleche, he withdrew a heavy beaded buckskin shirt that had belonged to some lost ancestor and laid it aside. It was too hot to wear it tonight, so he opted instead for the fringed leggings and a breechclout made of red tradecloth with tin cones sewn along the edges. He slipped his feet into moccasins, adjusted a quilled band around his arm and went back out.

The night was warm and sultry, with a frenetic undercurrent running through the crowd. It was impossible to look upon the encampment and hear the sacred songs and see the dancing and not feel his breast swell with the pride of being Sioux. The questions and uncertainties over which he had agonized in the sweat lodge seemed, for a few minutes, at least, small and far away—until he spotted Jenna standing between the lodges, her eyes glued to the flesh-piercing ceremony.

He shuddered when he recalled Sylvie's reaction to the sun dance, but he noticed that Jenna didn't close her eyes or turn away. On the contrary, she edged slowly closer, lured by what appeared to his watchful eyes to be a genuine curiosity.

His eyes stalked her as she moved among the lodges in those languid, graceful strides that made his throat go dry. She was wearing a long, loose skirt whose sheer gauze fabric showed the outline of her legs. A thin-strapped tank top exposed her flesh to the heat of the night. A wide silver bangle glittered from her wrist. He went to her, moving forward as if on strings manipulated by the unseen hand of his desire.

He stepped out of the shadows and joined her at the edge of the arbor.

"I didn't know if you would come," he said.

She turned naturally at the sound of his voice, as if she had expected him to be there. How many times had she looked at him and pictured him like this, looking as if he had just stepped out of one of her fantasies? In denim jeans, he was hard to resist. In tanned leather, he was breathtaking.

"It's all everyone's been talking about for weeks," she said. "I had to come and see it for myself."

But it was more than just curiosity about Indian customs that drew Jenna to the sun dance. She was curious about Trace's feelings for her, too. She had to find out where, in this world of drumbeats and mysticism, she belonged. Maybe there wasn't any place for her in Trace's world after all. Maybe she belonged back east, teaching underprivileged kids from the Lower East Side of Manhattan, who needed her perhaps even more than KayCee McCall did. She knew her teaching assignment at the Yankton Elementary School was only a temporary one, and that the day would come when she would have to leave. The thought was never very far from her mind.

Trace gestured toward the dancers and asked, "Do you want me to tell you about it?"

Grateful for a chance to get away from her unsettling thoughts of the future, Jenna answered, "Yes, please."

The fringe rustled along the sides of his leggings in the gentle night breeze as he silently observed the dancers, their chests glowing orange from the flames, red from the lifeblood spilled by the skewers. When he spoke, there was an edge to his voice, with what seemed to Jenna to be a chord of sadness vibrating underneath.

"For years it was banned, condemned by those who didn't understand." He gave a derisive snort. "Who are they to condemn something just because they don't understand it? It was revived in the thirties. Today, it's little more than a tourist attraction—a flesh carnival, if you will—in which the audience is invited to watch the spectacle of self-inflicted pain. But there it is, proof that my people's society continues to exist in spite of every attempt to stamp it out. You see, Jenna, we're as American as anybody else, only we're distinct, and that's what they don't understand."

He studied the perfect line of her profile etched against the night. Her face was bathed in the amber glow of the campfire. Her eyes were dark, like a deep green sea on a moonless night. He felt himself drowning in them.

"You're not frightened by what you see?"

"There's always something a little frightening about what you don't understand," she answered.

Like her feelings for this man, Jenna thought weakly. Who could ever understand what made one person attractive to another? Who could explain how or why her desire for this particular man exceeded all bounds? Was she frightened by it? Oh, yes. More than she'd been frightened of anything else in her life. Not even the sun dance, with its sacrifices of flesh, frightened her as much as her feelings for this dark-eyed man who stood nearly naked beside her, his smooth-skinned chest bearing no scars.

"You've never taken part?" she asked. Her voice was softly inquisitive, inviting his candor.

He shook his head. "The sacrifice weakens you. It takes a while to heal from an ordeal like the one these men are putting themselves through. I can't afford it. I need my strength to break mustangs. I've got a kid to support."

Filled with his own sense of what was right and what was wrong, he offered no apology for his choices. He was Indian enough to know that who and what he was was a part of something greater, yet man enough to create his own destiny by the choices he made. He was a rare combination of nineteenth-century belief and twentieth-century logic.

"What brings you here tonight?" he asked.

Jenna had come to respect his sense of responsibility and accept the arrogance that went along with it. "Just curious, I guess. The same as any other visitor. Although I will admit I feel a bit out of place, dressed so ordinarily."

But she wasn't the same as any other visitor, was she? And because of that, he hadn't been the same since the day he met her. "We can change that," he said. His hand found hers and enveloped its soft warmth in his.

Having learned a long time ago that it was easier to ask for forgiveness than for permission, he drew her forward, and led her away from the arbor, weaving his way back toward the far end of the crescent to where his mother's lodge was pitched.

He bent to enter, pulling Jenna gently along with him. Inside, he released her hand and knelt down at the entrance to position two crossed sticks outside in a sign for any who came by that those inside wished to be alone. Feeling as secure in their privacy as if he had locked a door, he got a small fire going in the center of the lodge, not big enough to throw more heat on the already warm night, just enough to let him see her beautiful face through the darkness.

The fire cast shadows across the canvas walls of the tepee. Overhead, where the long poles met, the smoke hole, browned by fires past, opened onto a starlit sky. He sat down on a pile of tanned hides, the pale light gleaming on his shoulders, and beckoned for her to sit down beside him.

They were facing each other, bodies not touching, yet each burning with the nearness of the other.

"Trace, there's something I have to tell you."

"Not now. Tell me later. There's something I want to see first."

He reached for something in the shadows. When he turned back to her, he was holding an eagle feather. Long ago plucked from one of the great birds by an eagle catcher, it had drifted down through his family as if on currents of air. He fastened the feather that had once adorned the head of some ancient warrior in Jenna's dark hair, positioning it hanging down, so that its quilled curve caressed her cheek.

In a reverential tone, he told her, "This is a symbol of bravery."

The feather grazed her cheek, lending an unmitigated wildness to her beauty. "But I'm not brave."

"Oh, but you are," he whispered. "To come here unafraid, to see all this and not to judge. You're the bravest woman I've ever met."

Starlight played across his naked back when he turned away again. This time he turned to her with a string of beads in his hand. He brought them up and over her head.

"These were given as a wedding present to my great-great-grandmother by her husband."

His fingers caressed the chevron glass beads as he slowly drew his hand away. He watched them rise and fall on an indrawn breath, then lifted his eyes to hers.

He leaned forward to kiss her, to say with his lips what a century of cultural clashes made it difficult for him to put into words.

Jenna drew back, a soft gasp escaping her lips.

"What is it?" he questioned. "What's wrong?"

Her head was spinning. Into her nostrils wafted the stirring scent of male musk and desire. She longed to quench the pandemonium he unleashed in her, yet she could not. She closed her eyes in agony and turned her head away.

"Oh, Trace, you can't put a feather in my hair and a strand of beads around my neck and pretend that I'm Indian."

"Is that what you think I want you to be?"

"Isn't it? You think if you adorn me in the trappings that you'll forget I'm white and that you've been hurt by a white woman in the past."

She saw his eyes flash at her through the darkness, and she knew she had struck a tender nerve.

"You talk about not being understood, about the wrongs that have been done to your people, yet in your own way, Trace, you're holding my differences against me. You're judging me based on past mistakes. You tell me you want me, but who do you really want—me, who I am, as I am, or some replica of something you wish I was?"

Trace felt as if he'd been slapped, again. She was accusing him of prejudice, and the painful truth was, she was right. He shifted uncomfortably, feeling indignant and trapped.

"What about you, Jenna?" he asked accusingly, abruptly turning the tables. "Your eyes tell me one thing, but every time I try to get near you, you run for cover. What gives, Jenna? What are you afraid of?

Not all relationships are as bad as the one your parents had, you know.''

She sucked in her breath sharply at having her innermost thoughts so blatantly revealed. ''Wh-what makes you think this is a relationship?''

''There's all kinds of relationships, Jenna. Maybe there is no right one, just the best you can do at the time. There aren't any guarantees. You should know that as well as I do.''

''It's not just that—'' she began. ''It's—''

''Jenna.'' His whisper was like a rough caress. ''Let me make love to you. I want you. God, you know I do. Can you look me in the eye and tell me you don't want me, too?''

He stared into her eyes, his own eyes deep, dark pools of emotion. ''Jenna?''

She couldn't do it. She couldn't look into his eyes and deny what she was feeling.

He sensed her surrender before he even saw it in the slight parting of her lips. He touched her cheek with his hand. This time he felt no resistance.

''Are you sure?'' he asked.

She nodded.

''I won't force you.''

''I know.''

''I can't promise you anything more than tonight.''

''I know that, too.''

His blood raced through his veins, testing the limits of his control. It would have been easy to take her in one mad rush, but he didn't. He wanted the thrill of every single moment as if it were his first, and to savor each one as if it were his last.

The air inside the lodge swam with the aroma of hides tanned to whiteness and the softly pungent fragrance of the sweetgrass Trace had thrown on the fire. He leaned toward her and pressed a kiss into her hair. Closing his eyes, he drew her scent deep into his lungs, filling himself with the essence of her.

Her mouth was waiting for him. He kissed her long and hard as he guided her down onto the hides. He shuddered, his body shaking hers, as well, with the power of his desire. He buried his face in her hair and whispered smoldering words against her ear, Sioux words that she didn't understand yet thrilled her with their intimacy.

He slid his hands to her shoulders and tugged at the thin straps there. The fabric fell away from her breasts, exposing the small, rosy tips to his hungry eyes.

"Beautiful," he murmured as he cupped them in his hands, scraping the swollen, tingling flesh with his calluses.

She felt the soft brush of his hair against her skin when he lowered his head and kissed one hard nipple, then the other, circling each with his tongue in lazy figure eights, then making her skin jump when his tongue slid to the sensitive undersides of her breasts.

His fingers were hard and possessive when they pulled the tank top up over her head and tossed it aside. They moved without permission or apology to the elastic waistband of her skirt and pushed it down over her hips and past her legs. His movements grew even more urgent as he grasped the lace of her panties and pulled them off.

A low growl of triumph escaped his lips when she lay beneath him on the hides, naked except for the glass beads around her neck and the eagle feather in her hair.

Jenna shivered in spite of the heat of the night, the warmth of the fire and the burning need of the man whose hands had stripped her naked. Whatever lingering doubts she had were obliterated by the raw, masculine power of him. It was easy to imagine herself powerless against him, to tell herself that she had no choice but to submit to his hard, driving hunger, that his callused hands would accept nothing less than her total surrender.

But the blood was sizzling through her veins, and when he lifted his head and looked at her with desire-narrowed eyes and demanded in no more than a whisper, "Tell me what you want," she answered, "You. I want you."

The little tin cones on his breechclout jingled softly when he lifted his weight from her and rose. With graceful movements that belied the blood rushing through his veins, he kicked off his moccasins. The fringe on his leggings rippled smoothly as he stepped out of them. She watched, mesmerized, her heart pounding as the breechclout fell away.

He was magnificent, a perfectly formed male animal with muscles that were clearly defined and bursting with unbridled strength. The flesh of his thighs was unblemished except for a scar in the shape of a half-moon where the skin had been ripped by the horns of a bull. His manhood was potent and throbbing in the firelight.

The hides dipped under his weight when he dropped to his knees and covered her body with the long, hard length of his. He touched her possessively, his strong fingers exploring all her intimate places before cupping the soft, dark triangle between her legs. There was a feverish need in his touch, despite the exquisite torture of his slow hand. He brought his mouth to hers again and kissed her deeply, probing the sweet wetness of her mouth with his tongue, filling her as his fingers filled her, urging her toward places she had never been before.

Jenna gasped. She felt alive, on fire inside and out. Her fingers tangled in the thick silk of his hair, feeling the dampness at the nape of his neck, pulling his mouth harder against hers, seeking to lose herself in his kiss as he breathed words she did not understand into her mouth.

"Mitawin. Mitawin," he repeated.

Her fingers splayed against the sides of his face, and she forced his head gently away. Breathlessly she whispered, "Speak to me in words I can understand."

But he was in control now. He shook his head and kissed her hard, sucking the breath right out of her.

The fire sputtered and grew dim, and the shadows shortened against the canvas walls that surrounded them. The August moon overhead was the only witness to the naked, entwined bodies on the bed of hides.

Jenna slid her hands to his smooth-skinned chest and felt the prick of his hard little nipples beneath her fingertips. She brushed her hands across rock-hard shoulders to the prominent muscles of his upper arms, past the quilled armband, the only thing he wore, down farther, to his flat belly and slim flanks, and finally to that place between his legs that was swollen with longing for her caress.

Her fingers enveloped him, stroking and kneading, exploring the rigid contours and unfurling a string of low, guttural moans from deep inside of him.

He grabbed her hand and pulled it away. His breath came in short, gasping bursts as his own hand took control, guiding the tip of his member along the inside of her thigh, setting the tender flesh on fire. Where his fingers had been before, he probed now, in and out of her delicate folds, all around that tiny peak that threatened to explode.

Jenna gasped with imminent pleasure, and twisted against him, longing for the feel of him inside her.

"Trace." Her voice was barely a whisper, thinning to a shuddering plea. "Now...please..."

"Soon," he answered, his own voice ragged and low.

He moved lower, planting eager, almost desperate kisses along her body. He loved the smell of her, the natural ambrosia that acted like an aphrodisiac to whip his male hormones into a frenzy. Her sweet, salty taste was more delicious than anything he'd ever had upon his tongue. He could feel her body straining under his deep, wet kisses, and it gave him a sense of triumph to know that he could possess her so fully.

He seemed to know the precise moment when she stood poised on the brink, and then his mouth came back to hers, wet and wild and tasting of her. His knees shoved hers apart and he sank into her.

Jenna gasped at the rough, rapid filling. Instinctively she began to move, meeting each thrust eagerly, moving with him in a heated motion, creating the friction that drove them both beyond reason. He slid his hands beneath her and lifted her hips higher, thrusting deeper, faster, his body pumping with unrestrained power.

It went beyond any conscious reason or thought. It was raw and basic. With a strangled cry of triumph, he exploded into her.

Mitawin. His woman. She was his.

There was only the sound of his breathing, rough and ragged as he lay atop the robes in a heated sweat, waiting for the world to return to normal. But just what was normal? Certainly what he had felt and thought before had no bearing whatsoever upon what he felt and thought at this very moment. If there had been any hope for him before, there was none now. In choosing to join his body with hers, he had irrevocably sealed his fate, creating destiny out of desire.

He remembered hearing a voice that sounded vaguely like his own, from some far-off place, saying, "I can't promise you anything more than tonight."

And now, he wondered, now that tonight was almost over, could he just pick up and leave as if it hadn't happened? As if it hadn't shaken him down to the depths of his soul and changed his life forever?

Jenna lay very still in his arms, her cheek nuzzled against his shoulder. A light sheen of perspiration glistened on her skin in the moonlight from above. In the aftermath of their lovemaking, she floated in a sort of dreamy reverie, half in, half out of sleep.

She had never been taken like that, so completely, so possessively. It was almost as if her surrender had not been voluntary at all, but taken forcefully by a man whose will was far stronger than her own, in a coupling that was thrilling and primal but without a word of love spoken, wreaking havoc on everything she believed about love and sex being inseparable.

There was a sense of contradiction in knowing that she could let him strip her bare of her clothing and her defenses and trust him to lead the way. It made her feel protected and vulnerable at the same time. Who knew to what heights he had the power to lead her, or to what depths, when next she opened her eyes and the dream turned back into reality?

She sat up and drew her arms across her breasts, hugging her shoulders. He had won. He had taken from her that which she had vowed never to give without love. She felt betrayed by her own emotions, a vanquished adversary in the battle they had waged from the moment of their meeting. She rose fluidly to her feet and went in search of her clothing.

Trace stirred and opened his eyes to almost total darkness. The fire had died out, and through the shadows cast by the moon on the canvas walls he watched her dress. She was so silky and graceful and perfectly formed, and he felt himself rising again with desire. Yet something in the taut silence that followed the rustling of her clothes told him not to reach for her.

His voice infiltrated the darkness to find her. "Where are you going?"

"It's late. I have to go." She didn't dare look at him. To do so would jeopardize whatever resolve she had left.

"Go where?"

Don't do this, she silently begged. Don't make this any more difficult than it has to be.

"Home," she answered.

He rose and came to her. "But it's still early. We have the whole night ahead of us."

Yes, she wanted to cry, the whole night. But what about tomorrow?

"I mean *home*. I'm going back east. That's what I tried to tell you before."

She'd known all along that when the school year ended she would have to make the decision of whether to stay or return to New York City. She'd been agonizing over it for weeks. Not until this very moment, however, had she realized that the decision had been made. With Trace unwilling to commit to anything more than a temporary longing, what was there to stay for, anyway?

"Leaving? Nebraska?" He was thunderstruck and trying hard to comprehend. His voice emerged as a hoarse whisper. "Why?"

"The fall term starts in a couple of weeks, and my assignment here is finished."

"I'm sure if you talk to the tribal council, they'd ask you to stay. They've been looking for a good teacher. I could speak to them for you. I could—"

"No."

"I know this place isn't Eden, Jenna. It's hot as hell in the summer and bitter cold in the winter. But you've never seen it in the springtime, when the prairie is blooming for as far as the eye can see, and the hills are alive with color. In a way it reminds me of you, wild and beautiful, and—"

"It has nothing to do with this place." The truth was, she'd come to love the hot, dry wind in her hair and the freedom of these wide-open spaces.

"Then what is it?" he demanded.

He knew in the awkward silence that followed that it was him. That she saw no future in the life he had to offer. Bitterness welled in his throat like bile. To have made this mistake once was unbearable. To have made it again was unforgivable.

In a voice taut with suppressed anger, he asked her, "When are you leaving?"

"At the end of the week."

So soon? He felt as if he'd been punched. "Do you need a ride back to your place?"

"No. I have my car."

He watched her turn and go, and long after she was gone he stood naked and alone in the center of the lodge, the stars shining down on him through the smoke hole, staring at the dark, lonely emptiness her going had left.

Chapter 10

There was a discernible difference in the light, a growing clarity that signaled the approach of another autumn.

In the dwindling light of a day in late August, Trace stood at the edge of the corral, watching the buckskin mustang pace the far fence. KayCee stood beside him, her arms folded on the middle post of the fence, her chin resting in her hands.

"Think he'll ever do things your way, Dad?"

"Think *you* ever will?" he tossed back at her.

At the elementary school, the summer session had ended and the regular term had not yet begun. Even though KayCee was still grounded for having run off with the buckskin, Trace hadn't been able to stay angry at her for long. She was too guileless, too pure in her actions, for him to think that she had disobeyed him for any reason other than that she thought it was the right thing to do.

Nevertheless, he had raised her to take responsibility for her actions, and despite the dissipation of his anger, he felt justified in doubling her chores and limiting her time watching television as punishment for having disobeyed him. Apparently she hadn't learned temperance as well as he would have liked, but he had only himself to blame for it, for he had taught her to be resourceful and independent, too.

It was too bad, he thought, that he had never been able to teach her how to withstand life's disappointments. He hadn't been able to ease the sting of her mother's rejection, nor had he recognized the pain caused by his own lack of attention. Of course, he hadn't wanted to admit that he was part of the problem. It was so much easier to blame Sylvie. Leave it to Jenna Ward to make him see the picture fully and not just from the lopsided angle from which he viewed it.

If only there were some way he could protect KayCee from everything, including himself.

And that horse.

KayCee was staunchly holding to her conviction that the buckskin had come to her rescue out of friendship. With her admission that she'd been sneaking out at night to feed him, Trace supposed it was possible for her to have bought the horse's friendship with treats. He watched the buckskin across the dusty corral. The horse did seem to calm down whenever KayCee was near. Who knew? Maybe there was something to it, after all.

He only wished there was something that could help calm his own anxiety. The thought of telling KayCee about Jenna had been causing him nothing but apprehension since the night Jenna told him she was leaving. KayCee had learned at an early age that life wasn't always fair, that it was filled with disappointment and people who leave. Now he had to explain to her why it was happening again.

"You know, kiddo, sometimes we have to let certain friendships go."

"You mean Buck, Dad? You're letting him go?"

"What? No, KayCee, that's not what I mean. I was talking about Jenna."

Relief washed over her face, even as her dark eyes looked up at him, inquisitive and faintly suspicious. "What are you talking about?"

"She won't be your teacher for the fall term. It was just a summer assignment. You knew that, didn't you?"

"Sure. But I heard that the tribal council was gonna ask her to stay."

"They did. She's leaving anyway."

He'd driven over to the seat of the tribal government the day after hearing the news that Jenna was leaving, prepared to argue with them in favor of her staying. He'd never expected to hear that they had already offered her a permanent teaching job at the elementary school, and that she had turned it down.

He'd been crazy to think that she would want to stay in a place like this. This was his world. It was hot and dry and inhospitable, but it was where he derived his strength. How could he think she would ever come to love it the way he did?

How could he ever expect her to understand what it was like for him, an Indian, in a white world?

The simple love of nature could never explain, for instance, what he truly felt for the land. It was more than his ancestral home, more than the root of his uniqueness, more than his identity. It was all these things, yet it was more. To him it was the measure of life. He denied the values placed on it by others. His own values were more eternal and essential to the human spirit, having existed long before the advent of barbed wire and commercial fencing. Even the badlands, where once the throbbing of drums had vibrated over the sagebrush flats, were beautiful to him.

How could he put into words that which beggared all description? Would Jenna ever understand? Coming as they did from two different worlds, the disparity between them seemed insurmountable. And yet, deep in his heart, he knew that if anyone was capable of understanding, it was her.

"But why, Dad? Why's she leaving?"

He didn't want to tell her that it was because of him. Why else would Jenna have turned down a job she obviously loved, if not to get as far away from him as possible? And why? Not because he was an Indian, but because he had made the dreadful error of not being able to promise her forever.

"It was just temporary, KayCee," he said, each word struggling harder than the one before it to get out. "She's got a life to get back to."

"It's not possible." He could hear faint chords of panic rising in her young voice. "She's so good for us."

"Us?" He nearly choked on the word.

"Yeah. The kids at school. We all like her. She does these neat things, like bringing in other teachers, our own people, Dad, who teach us the language. Some of the kids speak only English, and Jenna says it's important for us to know our own language. She said we should know the songs and the dances, too, but that we should also know about the Constitution, because it protects all Americans, and we're Americans, too. I remember once she told us that we're special because we're Americans and because we're something that few Americans understand. I'm not sure what she meant by that, but it made me feel kinda special anyway, you know?"

Yes, he knew. Jenna had a way of making him feel special, too, by accepting him for who and what he was without judging, by seeing him and only him. It made losing her so much worse.

KayCee looked crestfallen. "People are always leaving, aren't they, Dad?"

"Not everyone leaves," he said. "I'm still around."

"Yeah. And so's Buck. But Jenna's different. She knows how I feel deep down inside."

"I know, KayCee. I know."

He felt suddenly tired, and his body ached. The day after the sun dance, he'd begun his work with the buckskin in earnest. If he wasn't going to sell him to the rodeo—and he sure as hell wasn't going to turn him loose—he was determined to turn him into a cutter. He managed to stay on without being thrown, testimony to his skill in the saddle, but the animal still defied his authority and tried to nip him whenever he could. What with everything else he was contending with, his muscles ached as sorely as his heart.

"She likes you, Dad, I can tell. Maybe you could talk her into staying."

KayCee's childlike suggestion only compounded Trace's agony, bringing his angry frustration to the surface.

"Forget it, KayCee. Her mind's made up. I'm not a magician, for Christ's sake."

He saw the tears spring into her eyes and instantly regretted his harsh reaction. He slung an arm around her shoulders and turned her away from the corral. "Hey, look, I'm sorry. Tell you what—how about I cook dinner tonight, and you can have the night off?"

In between sniffles, a belligerent little voice asked, "And can I feed Buck some carrots?"

Trace looked down at his daughter. She was a smaller, more innocent female version of himself, stubborn and defiant to the end. He was too tired to fight it. "All right. You can feed him some carrots."

Twilight was tinting the western sky as they walked back toward the house.

Inside, KayCee set the table for two while Trace peeled and sliced the potatoes and plunged them into boiling oil.

"Hamburgers and french fries," he announced.

But not even the prospect of her favorite food could lure KayCee out of her sullenness. He tried a different tack.

"I was thinking that maybe we could drive down to Cheyenne for a couple of days. Your mom's competing in the rodeo there."

She shrugged, bravely trying to keep her tears at bay. "We don't have to. Besides, school will be starting soon, and Jenna says I need to brush up on my math."

Jenna. Was there nothing they could talk about that didn't lead back to Jenna? He slapped the chopped meat into patties, aggravated by the ever-present thought of her.

"I thought you might want to see your mom, that's all."

"I saw her a few weeks ago."

At times their sameness was a blessing, at other times a curse. Like him, she had come to accept Sylvie's absence from their lives. Like him, she'd been foolish enough to think they had found a replacement in Jenna. Like him, she was experiencing the sharp disappointment of Jenna's leaving. Unlike him, however, she didn't understand the full impact of it on her life.

With Jenna's help, KayCee was becoming a different little girl, right before Trace's eyes. The stubborn pride was still there, and the unwillingness to accept authority without question. She was still as outspoken as she'd always been, and just as precocious. But little by little the walls had begun to crumble and her guard had begun to slip, exposing the vulnerability that lay hidden beneath.

Over the summer, KayCee had come to trust the pretty green-eyed schoolteacher, enough to allow herself to be drawn out of her shell and to feel as close to Jenna as she might have felt to Sylvie if circumstances were different. He didn't know what they spoke about when they were alone, the private things Jenna confided or coaxed out of KayCee. He knew only that his daughter was somehow different and he had Jenna Ward to thank for it.

He watched KayCee load up her hamburger and french fries with ketchup. "How is it?" he asked.

Grudgingly she answered, "It's all right."

She blamed him for Jenna's leaving. He knew it as well as he knew that rain was coming when there wasn't a storm cloud in the sky. He could feel the tiny pinpricks of guilt over the part he had played in it. If only he hadn't come on so strong. If only he'd been able to let go of his bitterness long enough to see her for who she was and not judge her by his past mistakes. And now it was too late, and all the *if onlys* in the world made not one bit of difference.

He glanced up from his plate at KayCee, across the table. Her eyes were downcast and she was trying hard to concentrate on her hamburger. The sound of his own voice, pleading and desperate, surprised him.

"There's nothing I can do."

He was disgusted with himself for thinking that she could somehow absolve him of the guilt of his own prejudice. She was just a kid. How could she know what it was like for a man when he craved one special woman above all others and knew that her leaving would plunge him into a loneliness such as he'd never known before? Sylvie's leaving had never affected him like this. As angry and bitter as he was over it, he'd always known it was for the best. But this—this was different. This would leave a void inside him that he knew in the deepest part of his soul would remain aching and empty for a very long time.

Short of racing over there and telling her he loved her, what could he do? What if she heard his startling declaration and left anyway? The risk was too big to take. Or was it?

He could still hear her husky voice filling the silence in the cab of his pickup the night she'd told him that if he didn't risk anything, he wouldn't get anything back. The words still rattled in Trace's mind. But why should he risk everything, when it was obvious that she wasn't willing to do the same?

Trace cleared the table and dumped the dirty dishes into the sink. He washed them in silence as Jenna's words came back again and again to haunt him.

He'd risked an awful lot going to the rodeo that day, only to discover that he had blown it all out of proportion in his own mind. It reminded him of the time his mother had taken him to the movies for his birthday, a rare treat on any occasion. The preview for the coming attraction had been a clip from a werewolf movie. Being eight years old and unsuspecting, he'd sat there and watched as a figure darted from tree to tree, slowly advancing upon a cabin in the woods. When it popped out from behind the nearest tree into a close-up shot, he'd been scared out of his seat by the face of the werewolf.

For a long time, just the thought of that face had terrified him. Then, one night years later, he'd been at the local tavern with some friends and the same film had been on the television behind the bar. Unable to turn away and risk his friends' laughter, he had forced himself to watch, and as he did, a strange thing had happened. The face of the werewolf hadn't looked nearly as terrifying as it once did. He'd realized then that his fear of it had been blooming in the hothouse of his own mind.

In some ways, his reunion with Sylvie was the same. For five years he'd been brooding over their breakup and agonizing over the possibility that she might one day want KayCee back. It hadn't been until the day of the rodeo, however, that he knew his fears were unfounded.

Was that what this business with Jenna was all about, the old werewolf syndrome again? Maybe it was all his imagination, and her leaving had nothing to do with him. There was only one way to find out.

If you didn't risk anything, you wouldn't get anything back.

Suddenly it all seemed so clear. To hell with clashing cultures and past mistakes. Losing Jenna would be an even bigger mistake.

He shut off the water, wiped his hands on a dish towel and threw it on the counter.

"Get your things," he told KayCee as he headed for the door. "You're spending the night at your grandmother's."

"Where are you going?" she called after him.

"To get the pickup."

He knew that wasn't what she meant, but it was easier to answer only for the moment and not think about what he was going to do next, for the truth was, he didn't know.

He knew only that he couldn't let Jenna leave without telling her what he felt. Let her hear it, and then let her tell him that she didn't feel it, too. Let her, like him, experience the frenzy of going against everything you believed for something you could scarcely believe was happening to you.

Outside, gathering clouds obscured the face of the moon. The night air carried the faint scent of rain. A storm was threatening, but Trace paid it no mind. His thoughts were on one thing and one thing only. He'd never been a gambling man, but as he drove away from the ranch, headlights slicing two wedges out of the dark road ahead, he was willing to bet that a long shot at love was better than no shot.

Chapter 11

The hot bath Jenna had taken earlier helped ease the tension in her muscles, but did little to relieve the pain in her heart. With an absentminded gesture, she pushed back a lock of still-wet hair, pulled the sash of her robe tighter around her waist and cast a dismal look at the suitcase that sat on the bed.

Clothes sprouted from all sides of it, looking like something out of a Charlie Chaplin movie. She had put off packing until the last minute and now regretted it. How was it possible, she wondered, for the same belongings that had come west with her in early June to now refuse to fit in the suitcase for the trip back east? She begged, cajoled, and even tried sitting on the suitcase to get it closed, all to no avail. If her clothes wouldn't all fit into the suitcase, some would just have to remain behind. Why not? she thought with painful resignation. She was already leaving so much more than that behind.

Jenna turned her back on the suitcase and left the room, but while it was possible to avoid packing, she found that, try as she might, she could not avoid Trace McCall. He was there, everywhere, in her dreams, in her beleaguered thoughts. Even when not consciously thinking about him, she could feel the dark, brooding presence of him in the air she breathed.

In the living room, she went to the window and looked out into the growing darkness. How ironic it was, she thought, to have begun this odyssey disliking him for his arrogance and unapproachability, only to fall desperately and hopelessly in love with him.

Looking back, she could even name the precise moment it had happened. It had been the day of the rodeo, on the ride back to the ranch. He'd been driving with his arm around a tearful KayCee, consoling her with soft words spoken in their native Sioux language. It was then that Jenna had known beyond all doubt or reason that she loved him.

What had happened between them the night of the sun dance only complicated things. She knew he wanted her. He'd proved just how much that night. She had felt taken as completely as it was possible for a woman to be by the sheer force of a man's desire. But desire and love were two separate things, and what was one without the other? That night she had broken her own cardinal rule and flung aside everything she believed love to be for the incredible thrill of being in his arms for just one night.

The call from the tribal council offering her a permanent job teaching at the elementary school had only plunged her deeper into her agony. She loved it here—the children, the people, the wide-open space of Nebraska, the sizzling sun that had turned her skin brown. But it was the very thing she loved the most that had made her decide to leave in the end.

It was Trace. It was the hard, driving strength of his body on hers. It was losing her breath in the heated rush of his.

There was no denying the desire that raged between them, but that was just it. Animal desire was temporary, lasting only for the moment, and then the moment was gone. Was that what her relationship with Trace was destined to be, a series of couplings that left her breathless, yet always longing for more? It was best, she reasoned, to leave now, while she still could.

Leaving KayCee was just another painful consequence of her decision. Regrettably, it came just when she was making real progress with her. KayCee reminded her of herself at that age. The circumstances had been different, but the heartache was the same. KayCee was lucky, though. She had a grandmother who doted on her and a father who clearly adored her. And if Jenna felt more than a little bit guilty about leaving, it was because she had come to love KayCee, too.

She stood at the window for a long time, her fevered cheek pressed against the cool pane. Where were the stars that had witnessed her surrender only nights ago through the smoke hole of a canvas tepee? The sky was overcast and black. In the distance, a streak of yellow lightning illuminated the sky, followed by a far-off rumble. Jenna silently counted the seconds between the lightning and thunder. Ten, then nine, then eight. The storm was getting closer. So was the time of her departure.

Tomorrow she would drive to Omaha and board a flight for home. But where exactly was home? She was no longer sure. In the few short months she'd been here, she had come to regard this place as home. God knew, it hadn't been easy. She'd been a stranger, disliked by some, held in suspicion by others, merely by virtue of her not being one of them. But, gradually, she had won their trust, and learned the hard way that it was easier to gain the trust of an entire tribe than that of one stubborn man.

Overhead, the storm clouds looked like angry black fists clenched against the sky. The first drops of rain hit the glass in a gentle, deceiving patter, but within moments the full force of the storm was unleashed. The rain pelted the window like rocks, startling Jenna out of her somber thoughts.

She closed the blinds and backed away from the window, frightened by the fury whipping up outside. A terrible loneliness engulfed her, and despite the sheltering walls around her, she felt afraid. It was only a storm, she told herself. Just wind, rain, thunder and lightning, and that terrible banging from somewhere outside.

The noise heightened to a fearsome pitch. The front door shook from the pounding it was taking. At any moment, it seemed, it would burst open. Jenna cut a wide path around it as she rushed back to the bedroom. Midway there, she stopped. Was that Trace's voice she heard? Or was this just one of those odd times when the sound of his voice infiltrated her thoughts seemingly for no reason, as it so often did? She strained to hear above the rain, but heard only the pounding that continued from outside, until she could no longer tell if it was the external force of the wind or the frantic beating of her own heart caused by just the thought of him.

Above the wind and the rain, she heard his voice again, sounding so real and so near that she spun toward the door and was in motion before the realization even hit her.

He stormed in past her when she opened the door, then turned around and sharply demanded, ''What took you so long?''

He looked dangerously angry, with his hair dripping wet and his shirt and jeans plastered to his body. Puddles of rainwater formed at his boots as he stood glaring at her.

''I—I thought it was the storm,'' she said, faltering at the sight of him. He reminded her of a big tomcat, dripping wet and spitting angry. ''The thunder was so loud it shook the house.''

''It wasn't thunder,'' he said sourly as his obsidian gaze swept over her.

She looked utterly provocative, with her freshly scrubbed complexion still glowing from the bath and her hair curling in damp ringlets against the sides of her face. The robe she wore was of ivory silk, with a pattern of delicate lilacs. The slippery edge of the fabric fell a little past one honeyed shoulder. Her bare feet peeked from beneath its silken hem.

There was something odd in his gaze, something she'd never seen before. Jenna felt suddenly unsteady on her feet. "I see that now," she said nervously. "Wait here while I get you a towel."

His drenched and dripping state might have been funny, were it not for the fact that he was here, and she didn't know why. She hurried from the room. Out of his sight, she took several deep breaths, trying to pull together the threads of her composure.

She returned to him with a towel and a hopeless prayer that her emotions would not get the best of her.

His hair fell forward like silk-twined rope as he bent his head and rubbed it briskly with the towel.

She watched from a safe distance. "What brings you here on a night like this?"

From beneath the towel, he replied, "It wasn't raining when I left the house." He straightened up and began to unbutton his shirt. "I dropped KayCee off at my mother's."

"You must have known it was going to rain."

He had about him a way of knowing things by the movement of the air, the flight of the birds, a scent carried on the wind, things all but imperceptible to most people, but second nature to him.

Jenna's eyes followed as each button came undone, revealing his smooth-skinned bronze chest. He peeled off the wet shirt and ran the towel up and down each well-defined arm, over sinewy shoulders and across his muscled chest, movements working in harmony to create a symmetry of motion that trapped the breath in her throat. He was beautiful. It was a dark, wild kind of beauty, exquisite in even its imperfections, primitive in the effect it had on her.

It was only when his hands dropped to the zipper of his jeans that Jenna snapped out of the mesmerizing trance she was in, a trance caused by the handsome, nearly naked man standing in a puddle of water in the middle of her living room.

"Th-that's enough!"

He looked up, surprised by her reaction. Then a wickedly knowing little smile crept across his lips. "What's the matter, Jenna? It's nothing you haven't already seen."

Her cheeks flushed with embarrassment. Under the stars, cloaked in shadow and moonlight, was one thing, but in the broad light and reality of the room, while she was in control of her senses, that was another.

"Let's not play these games, Trace, all right? I'm tired and I have an early day tomorrow, and I'm still not packed. Why don't you just tell me why you're here?"

She was angry that he had the power to reduce her to the basest of emotions, and yet she embraced her anger, drawing it closer about her, like the folds of her silk robe, for in it lay her defense against him.

His hands dropped to his sides in a deceptively helpless gesture. "It's not easy to explain."

"Why don't you try?"

"You don't understand—"

"You're right, Trace. I don't." She gave a bitter little laugh. "I've been trying to understand you since the day we met, but you make it impossible. You've built a barrier around yourself so wide I can't bridge it. It's easier getting through to KayCee than it is to you."

"That's it," he said, a little too quickly, almost as if it had just occurred to him. "It's KayCee. I came here tonight to ask you to consider what your leaving will do to her."

A shadow of guilt swept across Jenna's face. "I know what it will do, but KayCee's a strong little girl. If she gets the proper attention from you, she'll be fine."

"You call that fine? Feeling like you've lost the one thing—the *only* thing—that matters?"

The almost desperate look she saw in his eyes made Jenna uncertain who he was speaking about, KayCee or himself.

"Children are resilient," she argued. "She'll bounce back, now that you've come to see what the real problem is. It's *your* love and attention she needs, Trace, not mine."

"So that's it?" His voice rose, and anger colored his hard-boned features. "You're just going to breeze into her life and breeze out again and kid yourself into thinking things will ever be the same?"

The same? God, no. Nothing had been the same since she'd met this arrogant man and his daughter and discovered just how much she loved them both.

"KayCee will be all right," she repeated, but she only half believed it herself.

"And what about me?"

She turned away from the uncharacteristic plea she heard in his voice. "What about you?"

Trace's throat went dry, and all the words he longed to say settled like dust upon his tongue. What emerged instead was an ultimatum he'd never intended.

"If you leave, Jenna, that will be the end of it. Don't expect me to come running after you. This is my world. It's where I belong. In your world I have no meaning, but this place, this is life to me. If there's to be anything at all between us, it will be right here."

She whirled around, shocked by his take-it-or-leave-it tone. "On your terms, you mean?"

"In this regard, yes."

His look hardened like steel, leaving little room for argument.

A taut silence ensued. When next he spoke, there was a carefully restrained tension in his voice.

"Did you know that no Mohawk has ever been buried in New York City? How many of them do you think lost their lives tightrope-walking the beams of the skyscrapers they helped build? All these years they've been going to work in the city, and all these years their coffins have been shipped home to the reservation in Canada for burial. There's only one reason why the Mohawks want to go home again. It's the land."

His face retained the same stoic look, but his coal-dark eyes blazed with the warlike belligerence of his ancestors. "The land of the Sioux has been dammed up, bled dry, flooded, stripped, eroded, leased out, wasted and legally stolen. But what looks like nothing but a dry, used-up patch of earth to you is life to me.''

The fires died, and something that looked like resignation flickered in his eyes. He shrugged and conceded, ''Still, I can understand if you don't like it here.''

''I never said I didn't like it here,'' she protested. ''There's something about this place that gets to you. There are no dress rehearsals here. Every day is the real thing. There's something reassuring in every sunrise and sunset, and yet it's so wild and unpredictable that you don't dare take it for granted. It's just like...''

Her words trailed off awkwardly when she realized she could just as easily have been describing Trace. Like the land, he was a wild and beautiful thing, hard and uncompromising, yet with immense reassurance in the strength of his embrace. A woman could feel protected by a man like him from everything except her own weakness. Even now she had difficulty bearing up under his silent scrutiny.

''What I mean is, I never said I...didn't...like...it here.''

''Then why are you leaving? Is it KayCee?''

''No! She's the sweetest kid in the world.''

His dark gaze burned into hers for a heartbeat, and in it Jenna saw his torment. His voice stretched tighter. ''Is it me?''

She swallowed hard, searching for an answer that made sense when none really did. ''It's just that New York is my home. It's where the opportunities are.

The wages are better, and I have my tenure to think of." But she knew in her heart that it was none of those things that had led to her decision to leave. It was Trace's unwillingness to offer anything more than the moment, and her own stubborn reluctance to compromise her feelings about love, even in the face of the strongest, most desperate desire she'd ever experienced.

Trace took a step toward her. "I need you, Jenna." His voice was low and urgent, his breath a harsh rasp against the quiet of the room. "Isn't that good enough?"

She lowered her lashes and looked away, remembering. "I knew two people once who thought it was enough, but it wasn't."

"Maybe not. Maybe it was sheer torture every step of the way for them. But something beautiful came out of it. You, Jenna. You came out of it. You're smart and resourceful and more beautiful than any woman has a right to be."

Caught up in emotion, he wasn't prepared for the way those green eyes flashed indignantly at him.

"I'm not having an identity problem, thank you. You're the one who seems to have the problem with who I am."

He stiffened as her barb hit its mark and twisted in his gut. He had come here tonight to tell her that he loved her, but what was the point, when it seemed she had made her choice, and he wasn't it? It was happening again, he thought with a harsh sting of regret. Just like Sylvie, she had chosen something more important than him and his child.

Jenna's voice sliced through the pain and the bitterness with nothing more than a whisper. "You still haven't told me why you came here tonight."

Trace wasn't sure who he was angrier with, Jenna for making a choice that didn't include him, or himself for being vulnerable to hurt over it. He felt himself backed into a corner, and like most wild things when trapped, he lashed out in a burst of anger that made Jenna's appear trifling by comparison.

"All right, damn it, you want to know why I came here tonight? Because I can't stand being without you. Because I crave the sight of you, the smell of you."

He spoke each word as if he hated the sound of it, his features twisting at the acrid taste of it upon his tongue. As he spoke, he came nearer, until his face was mere inches away and she could feel the furious rush of his breath against her cheek.

"Because all you have to do is look at me and I go weak all over. Well, except for one place, and that gets so hard sometimes I think it's going to burst."

Jenna's whole being flooded with hot embarrassment. She remembered only too well the silhouette of his potency against the darkness of the tepee. Her gaze dropped involuntarily to the press of his manhood against the tight, wet denim of his jeans. She looked away quickly. No! She wouldn't let him do this to her.

"What about you, Jenna? Don't tell me you don't feel it, too." He knew she did; he could see it in the scared look on her face. But he wanted to hear it. He *had* to hear it.

"Say it, Jenna. Tell me you feel it."

He wasn't giving her time to think, to shore up her defenses against what was coming. Damn him. Who was he to come here issuing ultimatums, telling her what he wanted and making her want it, too? Her voice sounded unfamiliar and far away to her own ears when she closed her eyes in anguish and said in barely a whisper, "What does it matter? I'm leaving in the morning."

"You can do that? You can just walk away?"

She opened her eyes and winced at the hurt and angry look on his face. "I've handled worse and survived." But she knew in her heart that it would never get much worse than this.

"Yeah, so have I," he said thickly. "Only I survived by taking what I need. And what I want."

He reached for her and hauled her hard up against him.

"Go on, Jenna, deny it. Deny feeling like you're drowning and the only thing that can save you is the very thing you're drowning in. Deny feeling an existence of yourself that goes beyond you. Deny that what you feel goes beyond pleasure to necessity, to the point where you're not sure where one of us begins and the other ends."

His eyes flickered with dark emotion as they searched hers long and hard. He didn't move, but the air inside the room was suddenly filled with the same static-charged intensity that had preceded the storm.

His voice was low and filled with dangerous desire. "And then deny this."

She made a small, startled sound that was muffled and then silenced against the crush of his mouth. Her body stiffened and sought immediate release, but even as she struggled against him, she knew she was beyond saving.

Chapter 12

He kissed her in a sudden, fierce rush.

The moment his lips touched hers, he felt the heat of battle flare inside him, where the desire to go slowly warred with the expedient need to take her all at once and tell her with every kiss and caress what was so difficult to say with words.

His muscles ached from holding his urgency in check, but with a will carved out of the same hard rock as the earth, he forced himself not to rush.

His hands slid up to cup the sides of her face, the tips of his fingers losing themselves in her chestnut hair. His mouth gentled and slid coaxingly over her lips. Slowly he invaded the warmth of her mouth with his tongue, savoring that incredible sweetness that had become like a drug to him. He felt her tongue rise to meet his, and a shudder convulsed him. Her hands slid hesitantly up his arms, raising goose bumps across his naked flesh, and came to rest upon his shoulders. He could feel the pressure of her slender fingers digging into his flesh, causing an exquisite pain that demanded no release.

He had wanted and not gotten many things in his life, but he was used to it. If anything, each disappointment added another veneer of protection and thickened his skin against those that would come. But what he felt for Jenna went beyond mere want. Somehow, someway, he had come to feel a need for her that went beyond the need for his next breath.

He could feel the pressure mounting. He couldn't control this much longer, he thought wildly. He couldn't contain this inferno she lit inside him without setting the whole place on fire. Somewhere in the last remnant of cognizant thought he told himself that it was possible that when this was over nothing would have changed, that she would still leave in the morning and he would still be faced with the long, lonely rest of his life.

He had to make this one count. The first time had been for him. This one would be for her, to drive her to the brink of madness, where he himself was teetering, to make her question everything that had come before and, like him, believe that none of it mattered.

His mouth left hers and trailed across her neck, pressing hot, wet kisses to the pulsing hollow of her throat. Her head fell back under the gentle onslaught, inviting the glide of his tongue along the outline of her collarbone.

With his dark head bent toward her, she surrendered to the impulse to tangle her fingers in the damp, heavy strands of his hair and pull his head ever closer, pressing his mouth tighter against her. She felt his body shudder and heard a low groan rumble deep in his throat. A small begging sound came from her own lips, but it was lost amid the pounding in her ears.

His hands slid over the silk of her robe like skaters on ice, down along her rib cage, tracing the outline of every bone beneath the smooth, taut skin, pausing at the outer curve of her breasts, thumbs flicking across nipples that were already hard with anticipation, before settling like two steel bands about her waist.

Her back arched in reflex, and he could feel the prick of her taut nipples brushing against him. He groaned again, but this time the sound was like that of a wounded animal, deep and guttural. His mouth returned to hers, tongue plunging deeply.

She gasped at the startling intimacy of his tongue searching the corners of her mouth, familiarizing itself with the dark recesses like a blind person exploring by touch. Her lips parted wider, welcoming the hot, moist breath that mingled with her own and the eager probing of his tongue.

Her silk robe seemed suddenly like a suit of armor, a heavy and unwelcome barrier to the feel of his hands on the flesh that waited naked and wanting beneath.

She was seized by a sudden, wanton desire to tell him what he wanted to hear, not to satisfy his need to hear it, but to put an end to the terrible pressure of keeping it inside. But her mouth was trapped in silence beneath the onslaught of his, and all she could do was show him.

Her fingers unlocked from around his neck. Her palms flattened against him and moved slowly downward until they came to rest upon the sensitive flesh of his chest. Her touch found the two dark circles and traced the outer edges that were puckered with readiness, her fingers teasing the hardened nipples within, stroking, caressing, tugging, inviting him . . . daring him . . . to return the brazen touches.

The blood pumped triumphantly through his body. Needing no further encouragement, his hands slid beneath her robe to claim the prize that waited.

She felt the scrape of his calluses as he cupped her breasts fully, enveloping them in the hungry knead of his hands. When he caught her nipples between his fingers, she cried out against his lips at the sweetness of the pain his overly eager touch inflicted.

His mouth released hers, and just as she sucked in a huge breath of air, she lost it again when his mouth claimed the breast his fingers had teased into throbbing awareness. He kissed one hardened nipple, then the other, drawing each in turn into his mouth, deeply, fully, leaving her skin wet and tingling in his wake.

Her hands were at the back of his head, pressing him to her breast as a low, protracted moan sprang from her throat. As she pressed him closer to her, she felt a pulsing need rising from somewhere deep inside, infiltrating every corner of her being. Yes, she felt it now, that frightening and exquisite sensation of not knowing where she left off and he began, the thrill of boundaries being broken and all limits surpassed.

The layers of her defenses melted away one by one, like icicles in the heat. Her anger dissipated, even that which she aimed at herself for this weakness that reduced her to a puppet in his arms. Beneath the defenses she had built to protect herself from loveless unions lay the desperate need for him that she could not deny.

He sensed it, and something surged inside him. She knew what he meant, and there was no longer any need to grope for words that would never accurately express this pandemonium he felt inside. There was no need to force the truth upon either of them anymore. It was there, bared to the fullest, open and aching and vulnerable between them.

Hunger. Desire. Lust. A score of words came to mind, all pitifully lacking when it came to describing what he really felt. Love, he thought wildly. He loved her. His aim had been to force from her an acknowledgment of her own need, and in doing so he had turned the tables on himself.

He growled against her breast. It was a low, harsh sound that sprang from the deepest part of his soul. Somewhere along the way, something inside him changed. Though it had happened in ways too subtle to detect, the savage need for possession was gone. In its place was a willingness to give up everything, even his deepest fears, to have the woman he loved. Not just for the taking, but for the giving. And it was that giving that excited him beyond all words. When all he'd ever done in his life was take what he could get, in her arms he'd learned how to give.

She felt the moment when he changed, when the desperate urgency in his touch turned to sweet eagerness. There was an almost shy, boyish quality to his kiss now, as if he were experiencing this ecstasy for the very first time. When he guided her to the hard planks of the floor, there was no force in his touch, just a gentle come-with-me urging. There was none of the harsh eagerness of before in the hands that untied the belt of her robe. With unhurried confidence, he slid the robe off her. It settled in a silken heap on the floor beside them, forgotten along with the remainder of his clothes which followed.

He stared down at her, savoring the sight of her that had previously been hidden by the shadows inside his mother's canvas tepee. His chest rose and fell rapidly, his expression that of a man who had only dreamed of such perfection and was now seeing it for the very first time.

"Jenna. Oh, Jenna."

The sound of her name, half moan, half plea, struck an answering chord within her own heart. Her previous reservations at being caught like this in the harsh light vanished. In truth, she craved the light, wanted it brighter, even, to see him fully in all his masculine beauty. There was the crescent-shaped scar high on his thigh that she had traced with her fingers previously in the darkness. There was that proud arousal that she had glimpsed in the starlight.

Whatever flush had spread over her at being naked before his heated gaze gave way to the even greater warmth of wanting him to see her, and to see in his eyes the raw nakedness of his hunger.

For several moments, all he could do was look at her, dark eyes drinking up her beauty with a thirst long denied quenching. He ceased his staring only when it hurt too much to look at her. Then he lay down beside her and, closing his eyes, drew her into his arms, her image imprinted irrevocably upon his mind.

He cradled her against him like some fragile thing that needed protecting, not daring to hold her too closely, for fear of breaking the most beautiful, delicate thing he'd ever had.

She had never felt so protected as she did in his embrace, or so cherished, and she smothered the joyful gasp that threatened to break the spell of the moment. The air was cool against her breasts, where the skin was still wet from his kisses. She twisted to move closer into his arms. Her nipples, chafed and reddened from the nip of his teeth, brushed against his, causing a muffled sound of pleasure to escape his lips. Without a word, she bent her head and began to press fervent little kisses against his chest.

Her movements stirred him beyond tenderness. He began to move again, this time with increasing urgency, raining hot, hurried kisses down on her as he covered her with the hard length of his body.

She writhed beneath him, her movements relentless, wreaking havoc on his control. With a boldness that thrilled him, she slid her hands along the broad muscles of his back, to his narrow waist, to the taut swell of his buttocks. She was pulling him tighter against her, fingers flexing convulsively against his warm flesh, wanting more, needing more, than the mere touch of their bodies. Nothing she knew had prepared her for the incredible longing she had to feel him inside her, to be a part of him in the most elemental of ways, to show him by their coupling how much she loved him when a stubborn and proud part of her refused to say the words.

She wanted to tell him, to whisper it into his ear, to shout it to the night, but her voice remained a mute, strangled thing in her throat. It was easier to admit her desire for him, because she knew he felt that, too. But what about love? Did he feel the same life-threatening love for her that she felt for him? He had confessed to so much tonight, but not to that, and a little jab of pain marred her perfect pleasure at the thought that, while he wanted her and needed her, he didn't love her.

Had there been any sane part of her left, she might have wriggled out of his embrace and put an end to this madness. But all she could do was feel, the incredible heat of his body, the bite of his swollen anatomy against her hip, the prick of his nipples grazing her flesh, and she told herself that nothing else mattered, not even the words she longed above all else to hear.

And why not? With every nerve ending writhing, with her blood screaming through her veins the way it was, why not cast aside every doubt, every misgiving, every preconceived notion she'd ever had, and live only for these few incredible moments? She was beyond caring that she was responding so fiercely. All she knew was that she wanted more.

She wanted every inch of him, every curve, every swell, of his beautiful body. Her fingers moved eagerly over him, across his back and down his sides, to the hardened curve of that muscle that fit so perfectly in the palm of her hand. She heard him gasp and felt his body go rigid the instant her fingers closed around him. The knowledge that she had the power to reduce him to such trembling emboldened her. Her hand began to move, stroking, sliding over his flesh with a maddening rhythm.

He was kissing her lips, her face, her neck, shoulders, breasts, making her tingle all over, filling every part of her with pleasure, except that aching hollow place that was yearning for him.

There was no holding back the moan that tore from her lips, half plea, half demand. "Please," she gasped. She wasn't even certain what she was pleading for until she felt his hand move to that warm, moist place that was waiting for him, open and ready. Her body moved of its own volition, legs parting, hips thrusting forward to give easy access to his probing fingers.

She cried out when his finger came to rest upon that tender bit of flesh and began a slow circular caress that drove her to the brink of insanity. He seemed to sense just when to stop, prolonging the exquisite torture until she caught a semblance of breath, only to begin again, proving that his mastery over her was an equal match to her power over him.

When the hot, demanding need threatened to boil over, he raised himself over her, his mouth seeking hers with desperate haste. Suddenly he tore his lips away as if he'd been burned. Bracing himself on his elbows over her, he looked down into her eyes. Her pupils were small, dark specks surrounded by a sea of green. Her sweeping black lashes were wet with tears.

"Jenna," he gasped. "Did I hurt you?"

She shook her head and reached for him, pulling his mouth back down to hers.

"I wanted to go slow," he whispered apologetically against her lips, "but you're driving me crazy."

"It's not that," she said breathlessly. "I've . . . I've just never felt like this. Oh, Trace, I don't know if I can wait any longer. Now, Trace. Now. Please."

Her name spilled from his lips, over and over and over again, mingled with words spoken passionately in Sioux that she did not understand.

He moved into the space created by her parted legs, hips molding to the curve of her hips, his male flesh probing her velvet folds. He meant to enter her slowly, gently, but the sudden flare of slick heat that met his sensitive tip jerked him forward with a guttural cry. With one long, hard stroke, he invaded her, severing the last thread of sanity that held them tentatively tethered to this world.

He lost hold of all restraint, thrusting with a furious rhythm, barely aware of the cries of pleasure that broke from his throat each time the entire length of him plunged into her. The slapping sound of their bodies meeting was obliterated by the pounding of his blood at his temples, her sharp little cries of pleasure lost amid the frenzy of his desire.

Through the narrow slit of her lashes, she saw his face above hers, handsome, rocklike, straining with emotion. His pleasure was both frightening and thrilling to behold. He was like a wild thing, filling her up completely, stretching her tender tissue with each savage thrust until she thought he would rip her in two. And yet she clung to him, binding the swollen male flesh to her and refusing to let go. He was hers for now, and even if she had no other part of him, at least she had this.

There were no tanned hides beneath her back now, only the wide planks of the hardwood floor. The light did not come from the fading embers of a fire, but from the harsh glare of a hundred-watt bulb. Those were not stars overhead, but the rough beams of the living room ceiling. Yet, as stark as it was, it seemed infinitely more real than that first time in the tepee, if only because the need that existed between them had no place to hide now. That had been a possession. This was a gift, not just from him to her, but also a gift he was allowing her to give to him and he was eagerly accepting.

In the full light of the room, she saw his face stamped with unbridled pleasure. At the sight of it, she cried out his name, and her body shook in exquisite convulsions.

In that instant, he froze, surprised by the sudden, violent contraction of her body. The realization that he had brought her to the brink moved him beyond pleasure, to something more primitive and basic.

With a hoarse cry, he exploded within her in long, throbbing thrusts. She locked her slender legs around him and moaned his name over and over again in breathless sobs, her lashes wet with a joy that was almost too painful to bear.

The pleasure seemed to go on and on, building in sweet fury to a shattering climax that left them both breathless.

Afterward, he lay atop her, feeling drained, his skyrocketing pulse gradually easing as the violent flow of blood through his veins began to slow. His breath came in quick, hot pants against the moist skin of her neck. He knew his full weight was upon her, but he could not move. Only when his pulse had stabilized and he could think a little more coherently did he withdraw from her velvet warmth and lift his weight off her and onto his elbows.

He looked down into her face. Her eyes were closed and her cheeks were bathed in the warm afterglow of lovemaking. He wanted to tell her so many things, like how grateful he was that she had helped him see the mistakes he was making with KayCee, how sorry he was for judging her, and how desperately he loved her. He wasn't at all surprised to discover that he, who had spent so much time shielding himself from this type of emotion, wanted nothing more than to bare it to her.

He wanted to tell her all this, but before the words could take shape, he felt her stir beneath him, and heard her ask in a sleepy murmur, "What was that word you said before?"

He nuzzled the tender flesh beneath her ear. "What word?"

"It sounded like *mitawin,* but I'm not certain."

With that one word, the reality of it all came crashing back to him. To admit its meaning would be to confess so much more, and she was right—what difference did it make if she was leaving in the morning?

He rolled off her and sat up, and she could feel the inexplicable bite of tension in the air. Had she said something wrong? It was only a word. Was it so meaningless that he didn't even remember saying it? Or, worse, did he regret it? She wondered what words she herself had uttered in those vulnerable moments bordering on delirium that she would regret now if she could recall them. But wasn't that what this type of thing was all about, abandoning yourself to the passion of the moment and saying things you would never otherwise say?

She rose to her feet, scooping her robe up from the floor in a fluid gesture. With a modesty that seemed almost ludicrous in light of what they had just done, she turned her back to him and shrugged into her robe, pulling the sash tight about her waist before walking barefoot to the window.

In a breath so soft that it left barely a trace against the pane, she said absently, "The rain has stopped."

"It always does," he said solemnly from across the room.

He pulled on his clothes, shivering at the coolness of the wet garments against his still-heated flesh. It was like throwing a bucket of cold water on a blazing fire. There was something sad and necessary about it. Yet, though it helped to extinguish the immediate flame, it left embers to smolder and burn a painful reminder through him of just how much he was losing.

He needed some air; he needed to escape from the confines of the walls around him. He'd always felt more comfortable outside, with the sky above him and the solid rock of the earth beneath his feet. He didn't need stars and full moons or the visual pleasures of the earth. Even if the sky was ink-black, obscured by thunder clouds as fierce as the ones that raged in his own heart, at least he knew it was there, somewhere above him, stretching to the ends of the world and taking him with it. Even if the earth was torn up by the hungry mouths of bulldozers, it was still there for him to walk upon. He needed the freedom of the sky and the earth as much as he needed his next breath, yet he made no move to seek it.

He felt rooted to his spot, unable to move, his stormy gaze riveted upon her from across the room. He could not leave, not yet, not when this might be the last time he saw her. Inwardly he went through the familiar motions of galvanizing himself against the inevitable.

"They say if you don't like the weather, wait five minutes and it'll change." He forced an uncaring note to his voice as he came to stand beside her at the window. "That certainly applies out here. Sometimes in winter the sky can be so blue it blinds you, and in minutes it begins to snow. Flurries can turn into a blizzard in no time, and before you know it, you're digging out from under eight feet of snow.''

"What do the horses do?" she asked.

"The wild ones fend for themselves. The ones at the ranch get put into the barn before it snows."

Yes, of course, he would know when it was going to snow by the feel of the wind against his face, wouldn't he?

"And Buck?" she wondered absently. "What will he do, I wonder, when forced into a barn this winter?"

"You're assuming he'll be around by then."

She looked at him then, turning her face slightly to see his profile, which was imprinted against the darkness beyond the glass. Surprised and hopeful, she asked, "You're going to let him go?"

"You think that?"

Her hope dimmed from his reaction. No, he wouldn't do that, would he? It was too much to ask for. It was too much to hope that he would let the mustang go and, in doing so, perhaps let go a little bit of his own bitterness.

"No, not really," she answered.

"Because I might sell him yet. No, not to the rodeo. Don't look at me like that. I promised KayCee I wouldn't, and I won't. But after I turn him into a cutter, I'll sell him for sure. That horse has caused nothing but trouble since the day I herded him in. It's best to get rid of him."

"It will break KayCee's heart."

"Aren't you the one who said she's a strong little girl? If she can get over you leaving, what makes you think she won't get over that miserable mustang?"

She had never backed down from him, and she wasn't about to now, in spite of the storm clouds she heard gathering in his tone, warning her she was broaching a dangerous subject.

"It's different with Buck," she asserted. "KayCee has connected with him in a way that goes beyond you and me. There's a real friendship there, Trace, whether you like it or not. Can you take that away from her?"

"What do you expect me to do? I don't need another cutting horse. I've got Teddy."

"Teddy is getting old."

He winced at the reminder. "I can get good money for the buckskin."

"You don't strike me as the kind of man who cares all that much about money, Trace, as long as you have enough to get by." It was one of the things she loved about him, his fierce independence from so many of the things that entrapped other men.

He turned fully to face her. "You want me to say it, don't you? All right, I will. I hate that damned horse. Not for what he means to KayCee—I can deal with that. But for what he represents to me. Freedom. Not just the freedom to run like the wind over the open prairie without a rope around his neck, but freedom from forethought, from apologies, from a past to regret. The freedom just to be. I hate him and I envy him, and I want him out of my sight, but I won't turn him loose."

She felt an overwhelming urge to put her arms around him and comfort him, because she knew it wasn't about the horse at all; it was about him. But she was afraid that if she did it, it might send him retreating behind the old shield of hostility. She stood there and said gently, coaxingly, "Trace, it's been a long time. Can't you let it go?"

He knew she wasn't talking about the mustang. She saw right past that, into his heart which was made of glass and so easily broken. She was talking about the unwarranted hold his bitterness had over him. The funny thing was, he had let it go tonight when, caught up in passion, he had abandoned himself to a greater emotion, one that centered solely around her.

"Sometimes I think it's possible," he said, but he failed to tell her that it was only when she was in his arms. "But you were right about what you said before. What does it matter?"

Had she really said that? And with the same chilling conviction she heard in his tone? She could feel the distance growing once again between them, and knew in her heart that she'd had just as big a hand in creating it as he did.

"There's just one more thing," he said. "I want to hear you say it. I want to hear you tell me that what happened between us tonight meant nothing to you."

"And if I can't tell you that?"

"Then I want you to tell me what you felt."

He could see the rise and fall of her chest, her nipples straining against the silken fabric of her robe as she drew in several deep breaths.

She spoke in a low voice, as if the words, spoken too loudly, would somehow mock the truth behind them. "I felt . . . whole. As if a part of me that has always been missing were suddenly restored. I want you, Trace. More than I've ever wanted any man. I'd be a liar to deny it. But I'd also be a liar if I said it's all that matters. Yes, your body fits perfectly with mine, as if cut from the same mold. Yes, you ignite inside of me a passion that I'm not likely to ever feel again. Yet neither of us can help being who we are. And no matter what passion we find in each other's arms, you'll always want just that, and I'll always need more."

Her eyes filled with tears, and she looked away quickly, partly to hide them from those dark eyes that missed nothing, but mostly because she could not bear to look at his face, which was stamped with such terrible hurt.

"Maybe you're right," he said. "Maybe that's the way it will always be between us. But if you don't risk anything, you won't get anything back."

Jenna froze. It seemed years ago that she had said the very same thing to him. She resented having her own words flung back at her, yet could they be any less true for her than they were for him? He'd had the courage to put that risk to the test. Did she?

Trace didn't want to make this any harder than it had to be, but he couldn't resist the temptation to reach for her and pull her roughly into his embrace. Smothering his face in her hair, he asked, "Do you want me again?"

She made a small sound of acquiescence.

"Because I want you." He lifted her into his arms as if she were made of nothing more than air. "Which way?"

She nodded shyly toward the bedroom.

He muttered something indistinct as he carried her across the room.

He laid her down on the bed and with a fierce kick sent the suitcase to the floor as he covered her body with his.

This time there were no preliminaries. His body surged into hers with the old familiar possession. She clung to him, her head falling against the pillow with the first furious thrust, her cries lost somewhere in the tumult of those words coming back again and again to haunt her.

If you don't risk anything, you won't get anything back....

Chapter 13

The geese were coming out of the north country and heading for the Platte in vee-shaped formations that contrasted with the crystal blue of the sky. The prairie was covered each morning by a blanket of frost that was gone by the time the sun was high. Into the charged stillness of the September air, the high-pitched whistles of the bull elk could be heard rising from the breaks.

In the west corral, Trace had just finished putting Teddy through his paces. The big sorrel still possessed the grace that had always come naturally, but his stamina was suffering the effects of age. Trace no longer galloped him hard over the open plains. Teddy's activity these days was limited to cutting maneuvers in the corral and playful romps in a field of clover just south of the house. Trace had toiled all through the remaining days of summer to erect the fence that surrounded it, first scouring every inch of the land on foot for signs of gopher holes. That was where he led the horse now.

He reached up and removed the familiar bridle. He'd lost count of the hundreds of times over the years that he had put it on and taken it off that pretty white-blazed face. The thought that one day he would no longer do so threw him into a discomfort so inconsolable that he forcibly shoved it from his mind.

He didn't want to think about Teddy's demise, because it only made him aware of his own. It wasn't death that frightened him, though. Death was just another part in the circle of life. It was neither the ending nor the beginning, only a necessary part, like living, although there were times when his heavy heart wondered at the necessity of that. No, the thing that frightened him most was the long, lonely hours, days, months and years that would precede it. That night three weeks ago, when he walked out of Jenna's house, and her life, forever, he'd been convinced that his own death was somewhere far in the future, and that each day lived from then on would be the longest and loneliest of his life.

He'd manufactured dozens of excuses to justify what happened between them. They were too different. Or they were too much alike. One moment it was his fault; if only he'd been friendlier at the start. Then it was hers; if only she hadn't been so stubborn. He passed his days heaping blame upon himself for his mistakes and damning her for letting hers keep them apart, all the while wanting her and hating himself for it.

KayCee had reverted to her former sullen self. Jenna's leaving had hit her hard, too, but instead of turning an embittered heart against it, Trace found himself seeking his daughter's attention, as much for her sake as for his own.

She'd be home from school soon, and he looked forward to seeing her. When she was around, she helped ease the loneliness. It was only when she was at school, or in the middle of the night, when he sat with his back pressed against a pine tree in the grove near the house, that nothing could ease the pain of his own mistakes.

He watched the sorrel sprint to the far end of the clover field, its red coat sparkling in the sunlight. There was one more thing he had to do, and he went off to do it, hoping to get it done before KayCee got home from school.

He didn't need her petulant, doleful looks whenever he worked with the buckskin, or that defiant look behind her eyes that reminded him way too much of himself and told him she was up to something.

Trace had hoped that, with the start of the new school year, KayCee would be preoccupied with schoolwork and friends and would give up pestering him to turn the horse loose, but she hadn't. The thing she seemed to lose interest in instead was school.

When he questioned her on it, she exclaimed that it just wasn't fun anymore, that it was all hard work, that the new teacher was mean and yelled at the kids when they didn't learn their lessons, that she hated school and was never going back. In the end he convinced her that it was in her best interests to go back on her own, that if she didn't it would be a long time before she was able to sit on a horse comfortably—or a chair, for that matter.

They both knew the threat was meaningless. Among the Sioux, it was believed that adults should never take out their aggression upon their children. But KayCee was too old to influence easily with common frighteners like the owl or the *cici*-man to persuade her to obey, so he resorted to the empty threat of a spanking and a take-it-or-leave-it look on his face to persuade her to return to school.

But she no longer showed the same enthusiasm for school as she had over the summer. Not two weeks into the new school year, and her grades already showed signs of slipping. Where was Jenna when he needed her? He knew beyond any doubt that it was Jenna who had made the difference. *She* had made learning fun for KayCee. It wasn't just KayCee who lost something important with Jenna's going, but every other child in the class. Would she come back if she knew how much those children needed her? If she knew how much *he* needed her?

He liked to imagine that she was considering it, but then the truth would blur the foolish notion. He knew that she wanted him to follow her. How many times had he come close to hustling KayCee off to his mother's and doing just that? But no! As surely as he lived and breathed, that place from which the sun rose was not for him.

If she really wanted the modern facilities and better wages the city had to offer, why had she ventured to his godforsaken corner of the earth in the first place? Judging from the nonconformity in her nature that had brought her there, he knew that place back east wasn't for her, either. This was where they both belonged, but only he seemed to know it.

Buck pitched his usual fit before settling into an irritable trot around the corral. Trace kept him under a tight rein, knowing that the horse would take advantage of the slightest weakness, either in rein or in rider, to toss Trace from his back. No love was lost between those two, yet as the days of autumn grew shorter, Trace and the buckskin mustang had formed a grudging team with one thing in common. Neither of them liked the other.

The buckskin was a rapid learner when inclined. By this time he was cutting corners as if he'd been born for it, his speedy hooves rustling the leaves that had fallen from the trees and been blown into the corral on gusts of wind. Trace had it in mind to speak to a man who sometimes bought stock from him. He had a spread of more than four thousand acres in Montana and over two thousand head of cattle, and well-trained cutting horses were essential to him. Buck would bring a good price, provided he could keep his evil temper in check and not incite his new owner into loading him into the trailer and transporting him back to Nebraska for his money back.

The ensuing hour was hard-fought, but in the end Trace managed to teach the ornery mustang a few new tricks. Unhampered by a wristwatch, he took a quick glance at the sun that told him that KayCee would be home soon. He ought to have stopped his work with the buckskin for the day, but it was going too well. Sometimes it seemed the animal learned out of pure spite, but whatever caused it, Trace wasn't about to pass up an opportunity to teach him more.

Things were going well until some sort of internal alarm clock went off suddenly inside the horse and the lessons came to an abrupt end. No matter how hard Trace tried to force the issue, the buckskin resisted. As it so often did between them, it came down once again to a battle of wills.

Trace jumped from the mustang's back and left him saddled in the middle of the corral to let the horse think things over for a while. He snapped the red bandanna from around his head and whipped it against the side of his lean-muscled thigh as he stalked out of the corral. He'd win with that damned animal, or he'd die trying. He wasn't about to suffer another defeat.

A lock of jet-black hair sliced his face as a gust of wind swooped down from the high places. He could feel the chill against his cheek. Winter was coming.

For the past five years, he had looked forward to its coming. When conditions were at their worst, he would pack KayCee up and drop her off at her grandmother's so that his mother had company and KayCee was closer to school. For days and sometimes weeks, the only voice he heard was his own. There was a certain comfort in the stillness, a solace in the silence created by a thick blanket of snow. But this time was different. This time he dreaded the thought of being isolated...of being alone. How could he ever go back to that solitary time before Jenna had come along to change everything?

At the sound of a vehicle approaching, Trace turned and saw the yellow school bus rumbling down the road, its exhaust rising like smoke signals against the blue sky. But the smile dropped from his face when the bus didn't stop to let KayCee off. Every day she got off that bus like clockwork. Where was she? A panicky feeling began to churn in his gut, slowly working its way to his heart to make it beat faster. KayCee was stubborn and independent, but she wasn't foolish enough to run away. Or was she?

Trace was already in motion, racing back to the house. He bounded up the porch steps and stormed inside. His fingers shook as he dialed the number of the elementary school. The panic he felt turned to downright fear when the voice at the other end of the line confirmed that KayCee had not shown up at school that day.

He hung up and dialed his mother's number, but before her phone even rang, he slammed the receiver down. If KayCee had shown up there, surely his mother would have called to let him know. And if KayCee hadn't shown up there, what was the point in causing her the same distress he himself was feeling?

His breath was coming now in rapid bursts as he dialed the number of the reservation police. In a tightly controlled voice, he explained the situation and answered their questions.

"About half an hour ago. That's when she should have been home. But I'm telling you, she wasn't at school all day. What do you mean, twenty-four hours?'' Outrage added to his growing panic. "She has to be missing twenty-four hours for you to do anything? Yeah. Right. Whatever you say.''

He slammed the receiver down and glared at it as if it were his enemy. For the first time in his life Trace felt truly scared. But, scared or not, he wasn't helpless. If the police couldn't do anything for twenty-four hours, he sure as hell could.

He pivoted sharply on his bootheels, thoughts whirling madly as he stalked to the front door. With one angry burst, the screen door flew open on its hinges and battered against the house. The wide, rough planks of the porch shook under his angry, determined stride as he made his way across them. He got to the top step and was about to descend when his head came up and he stopped short. The breath went out of him all at once. There was KayCee, standing not twenty yards away.

Relief overwhelmed him at the sight of her. He wanted to yell at her for the worry she had caused him and hug her desperately close to him, all at the same time. He descended the steps, assessing her as he approached.

"I was just about to get into the pickup and come looking for you. You weren't at school today. Do you want to tell me where you were?"

KayCee bit her bottom lip to still its trembling. She swallowed hard, but before she could utter a sound, a familiar voice spoke from off to the side, and a figure he hadn't noticed before stepped forward.

"Hello, Trace."

It was Jenna, looking just the way she had the first time he saw her, dark hair brushing her shoulders in the stiff breeze, green eyes fixed cautiously but straightforwardly upon him.

There was no place he could look these days without seeing her face. It was there among the clouds, etched upon the floorboards beneath his feet, gazing up at him from his morning cup of coffee, and around every corner. But with a start he realized how pitifully wanting his wildest imaginings of her had been, compared to the real thing standing before him.

He wanted to run to her, take her in his arms and kiss her, but there was no guarantee that he or his kiss would be welcome. He recognized that look on her face, the one that beckoned him and warned him to keep his distance at the same time.

He came forward, his animal grace a natural concealment for the pandemonium that ripped through him, caused by her unexpected presence. He forced himself to walk right up to her.

"What's going on?"

Jenna saw the vestiges of worry on his handsome face and knew what he must have been going through. Still, there was no easy way to say it, so she opted for the simple, honest truth.

"She's been with me."

"All day?"

"Yes. I planned on getting her back here on time. We didn't mean to worry you."

"Well, you did. And you—" He turned his angry attention on KayCee. "What's this all about?"

KayCee's dark eyes shifted toward the corral around back.

Trace understood immediately. "Don't start, KayCee. I'm in no mood. As long as I pay the bills around here, I'll do what I think is best. And if it means turning that buckskin into a decent cutting horse, then that's what I'm going to do. And I want no more arguments about it from you. Are you clear on that?"

The last thing he needed was to feel guilty over the buckskin. He had learned the hard way what happened when you let your emotions overrule your logic. This was business, he told himself.

KayCee's bottom lip jutted out in a pout, and she looked so doleful that Trace regretted his temper. It wasn't her fault he was in such a dark mood lately. If anything, she was the only thing that brightened his days.

"Why don't you go inside and change your clothes and get started on your chores? We'll talk about this later."

KayCee looked back at Jenna and hesitated.

"I'll go in with her for a few minutes," said Jenna. She moved past Trace and took KayCee by the hand, and the two of them disappeared inside the house.

Trace rolled his eyes as he watched them go. He'd get to the bottom of this later. Right now, he needed time to think. He headed for the crooked path behind the house and climbed it to the top of a rise, where he stood for many minutes with his feet apart and arms crossed over his chest, gazing at the panorama spread out before him.

There was a hypnotic quality to the long, even stretches of land. He'd have been hard-pressed to convince people from other regions that endless miles of prairie could be beautiful, that flatness had an appeal of its own, but it could and it did. The hills in the distance would soon be covered in saw-toothed patterns of snow that would linger long into spring, but for now they wore the softly muted tones of autumn that came in the weeks before the leaves turned fiery-bright.

The sight of it filled him with old familiar memories of the autumns of his youth, when he used to steal pumpkins from his neighbor's patch because his family didn't have a patch of its own.

He remembered the chilly daybreaks when his mother would shake him awake to do his chores before school, and the cold autumn evenings sitting in front of the fire, listening to her tell the stories and myths of the Sioux. She used to tell him that it was because they were Indian first and all else second that they had survived as a people, and that one day his heritage would be the means of his survival.

All in all, he considered himself a lucky man. He made a decent living. He had a daughter he loved beyond reason, in spite of her rebelliousness, and a mother whose stories on cool autumn nights still warmed his heart. There was just one thing missing.

For years he had brooded over the absence of something he felt down to his Indian soul yet had never been able to define. He'd been foolish enough to think that marrying Sylvie might help ease that inexplicable longing, but it hadn't. It was always there, lurking like a phantom in the deepest part of his heart, that nameless, faceless thing that left an unexplained emptiness in its wake.

It hadn't been until he met Jenna Ward that he realized what it was. It was the need he had not only to love a woman, but to be loved back, for no other reason than that it was meant to be. With Jenna he had come closest to realizing that thing that had remained undefined for so long. But the joke, it seemed, was on him, for coming so close, only to be left with the familiar aching need. Only now it had a name. Its name was Jenna.

The pain of losing her was almost physical, yet if he had a choice between feeling the pain or nothing at all, he would choose the pain, because at least it meant that he was alive and not the unfeeling thing he had been before knowing her.

His arms fell with resignation to his sides. He drew a breath of crisp, clean air deep into his lungs as his dark eyes swept the horizon one last time before turning away. He took no more than a step and froze.

Jenna was standing there, looking so damnably beautiful with the wind whipping through her loose hair, her eyes looking even more green in the sunlight.

He walked up to her and right on past, saying, "I thought you were leaving."

Jenna hadn't expected a passionate welcome, not after the way they had parted, but his icy demeanor sent a chill down her spine. All the speeches she had rehearsed, all the little tricks she had used on the way over to boost her confidence for this meeting, fled from her mind as she walked with him down the crooked little path that led back to the house. She had to walk fast to keep pace with his long strides.

"I changed my mind."

There was a slight trip in his step. His gaze darted to the ground, even though he knew his misstep had been caused not by a twig or an upturned root, but by a sudden surge of joy from within.

"You mean you're staying?"

"Yes, I am. I've spoken to the tribal council and agreed to stay for at least another term. They gave me a couple of weeks off so that I could make arrangements to sublet my apartment in New York and have the rest of my things shipped out here."

"When did KayCee find out you were still here?" he asked.

"They made an announcement at school yesterday."

KayCee had known since yesterday and hadn't told him? What was this, some kind of conspiracy? His anger over it showed when he asked, "What changed your mind?"

She answered sincerely, "KayCee."

"I knew it," he said. "I knew you were no coward."

Her gaze touched his briefly before seeking refuge amid the scattered leaves at her feet. Softly she confessed, "Maybe I am, because I'm scared to death."

Trace looked at the top of her dark head, which was bent at a shy angle, and asked, "Of me?"

"Of you. Of me. Of this place, sometimes."

Neither of them was aware that their steps had slowed, nor had they expected her painful candor to bring them to halt in the middle of the narrow path.

"I hadn't planned on coming by. I didn't think it would be a good idea for us to be together and perhaps give KayCee the wrong idea."

She had stayed because, in spite of everything, she couldn't give up on KayCee. But Trace was a different matter. It took courage to admit to herself that the mere act of breathing had become difficult without him, yet she also could not forget the night of the storm, when he had admitted to everything except loving her. Without any hope for a commitment from him, there was no point in giving KayCee any false hopes.

"You don't have to explain," said Trace. He felt foolish enough for thinking that her staying might have had anything to do with him. "I don't blame you for not wanting to see me."

An awkward silence settled in between them when they resumed walking.

At the house, there was no sign of KayCee in the kitchen.

"She must be upstairs changing her clothes," said Trace.

Jenna looked away nervously, embarrassed by the lust she saw in his eyes, which he could never quite disguise. "I saw Buck saddled in the corral when we drove up."

Trace walked to the sink and turned on the tap. "He's thinking things over. In time he'll come to learn that I'm the one who's in control."

Control? That was a laugh, he thought with disgust. He'd been careening out of control since the first time this woman walked into his life, and here she was again.

Jenna stood in the doorway, watching the muscles flex in his back as he washed his hands beneath a stream of tap water. She hadn't expected his feelings about her to change. After all, hers hadn't; she still believed that love was forever. She had hoped, however, that he would be able to put the old bitterness aside and turn the horse loose.

She remembered what he'd said once about old habits dying hard, and observed dispassionately, "I guess some things don't change."

He turned to face her, leaning back against the counter as he dried his hands with a dish towel. "No, Jenna, some things don't. Like this burning need you churn up inside of me."

Unprepared for the impact of his candidly uttered confession, Jenna fought to regain her composure. "KayCee said she has a surprise to show me. Do you know what it is?"

"Beats me. Maybe she's changed her mind about that horse. Now that would be a surprise."

His remark brought a disapproving look. "How many times do I have to tell you? She'll—"

"I know," he told her. "She'll be all right."

"And all it takes—"

"Is my attention. You see how I've learned my lessons, teacher? Do I get a gold star, at least?"

He smiled that rare, devastating smile of his, and for a moment she felt herself weaken under its brilliance. If he'd reached for her then, she would have forsaken everything just to be again in his arms, but he didn't. He just stood there leaning indolently against the kitchen counter, staring at her with those intense black eyes that had the ability to see right through her, smiling as if to say, "I know why you really stayed."

Nothing in Jenna's demeanor bothered to deny it. He would have seen right through her if she tried. It was easier to acknowledge it than to try to hide from it. A single look passed between them, and in that moment all pretense was dropped.

Her voice came softly from the doorway. "I don't know if I can give you what you want."

"And what is it you think I want?"

She didn't flinch under his stare, but something inside of her quivered. "I think you want only the moment."

"What's wrong with that?"

"Nothing. If you believe only in the moment."

"But that's all there is, one moment following another, just as one season follows another, and it all forms one big circle. That circle is life, Jenna, so don't ever underestimate the value of a moment."

Tossing the dish towel onto the counter behind him, he came forward. He moved past her through the doorway and walked out of the kitchen, leaving her standing there in choked silence.

He returned a few minutes later.

"She's not upstairs. She probably got started on her chores. I'm beginning to wonder if that big surprise she told you about wasn't just a ploy to get the two of us together.''

"I guess we might as well get used to the idea that we're going to run into each other from time to time," said Jenna.

His voice was low, the grumble in it unmistakable, as he started for the door. "I'd sooner get used to being struck by lightning."

Outside, the breeze picked up, swirling leaves in eddies at their feet. Jenna wrapped her arms around herself as they walked to her car.

"Didn't you bring a jacket?" asked Trace.

"It was warmer when I started out."

"The weather out here is unpredictable," he said. "You'll get used to that. Until then . . ." He shrugged out of his denim jacket and held it out for her.

"Trace, there's no need . . ."

"Take it, would you? Your teeth are starting to chatter, and your...uh...your..." His eyes fell with instinctive male appreciation to the natural reaction of her nipples beneath her blouse. "You just look like you can use it."

She turned her back shyly and let him slip the jacket up over her arms and onto her shoulders. The fabric was soft from wear and warmed by the heat of his body. The scent of him clung to it, filling her head with memories of their intimate moments together, when she had breathed the intoxicating essence of him into her being. The remembrance sent a chill down her spine that had nothing to do with the cold snap in the air.

His hands lingered at her shoulders, their touch like hot irons that seared clear through the faded denim to scorch her skin beneath. She flinched away from him.

His fingers withdrew reluctantly. "I can't imagine where KayCee disappeared to."

"Maybe you were right about her matchmaking efforts," she said. "If you like, I'll explain it to her."

"Explain what?"

"Why you and I aren't...why we can't be together the way she would like us to."

"Yeah? Then maybe you can explain it to me, because I sure as hell don't understand it, either."

"What I meant," she said, straining for patience, "is that I would speak to her as..." She stopped when she saw an unreadable look spring into his eyes.

"As what, Jenna? As one woman to another? What does KayCee know about being a woman? She's only twelve, for Christ's sake."

"Of course not. But I was her age once, and I know what *that's* like."

"As what, then? One child to another?"

"Don't be ridiculous."

"As one female to another?"

"Hardly anything so clinical," she protested.

"As teacher to pupil?"

"Well, yes, that, but..." It was more than that, so much more that she was afraid to put into words.

"But what, Jenna?"

It was no use to try to evade him. Those wolflike eyes had sighted their prey, and stalked it now with a long, steady look.

"I've grown very fond of KayCee," she said. "More than fond, in fact. Probably not the wisest thing, considering the circumstances, but there it is."

"And what are the circumstances?" he said with a laugh. "That we're crazy about each other?"

"I'm glad you can find some humor in it," said Jenna. "It's better than that other thing that prevents you from letting that horse go."

His laughter died suddenly, like a fire doused with water. "What other thing?"

"That bitterness you carry somewhere in there." She pointed accusingly to the spot where his heart beat rapidly in his chest. "You wear it like a shield. But haven't you heard, Trace? The Indian wars are over. Maybe you ought to put an end to yours, as well."

"Are you trying to teach me another lesson, teacher?" he asked, his voice softly menacing.

"I'd sooner try to teach an old dog a new trick," she replied. "At least I'd have a chance of succeeding. The praise-and-reward method works wonders, I hear. You might keep that in mind when you're working with Buck, since you're so determined not to turn him loose."

"I like to think I'm more determined to keep him."

"Is there a difference?" she questioned.

"You know, Jenna," he said, "we Sioux have this belief about doing what you feel is right for yourself and answering to no one but your own inner voice. You're right about the mustang, but I'm not losing any sleep over it. If I have trouble sleeping, it has nothing to do with him. And it's not about Sylvie, either. At least not anymore. If I lose sleep at night, Jenna, it's because of you.''

"That's not fair. I lose sleep at night, too, Trace, but I'm not blaming you for it.''

"Really? Then whose fault is it?''

"It's *my* fault, Trace. All right? My fault for getting involved in the first place.''

"Then why'd you do it?''

"I had no choice.''

"Right,'' he roughly agreed. "And neither do I, where that horse is concerned.''

"People can't help their emotions,'' she said, "but you can certainly help what you do with that horse.''

"Why is that damned horse so important to you?''

"Because it's important to KayCee. That's why she came to see me today. I guess she feels she has an ally in me where Buck is concerned. And in answer to your question, I would talk to her as one human being to another, because that, after all, is what we are.''

He'd been hoping she was going to say as a mother to a daughter, but when he heard her answer he knew that what she offered was even better. Never mind that he was a man and she was a woman, or that he was Indian and she was not, or that she was an adult and KayCee was a child. What feeling or emotion was so unique to the human spirit that others didn't feel it, too? As different as they were, their humanness made them equal.

"You don't have to explain anything to KayCee,'' he said. "She's my kid. I'll do it.'' He looked around and wondered aloud, "Where is my kid, anyway?''

His gaze strayed to the house, to the window of his daughter's bedroom, on the second floor. "She usually goes straight upstairs after school to change her clothes." He turned his head toward the barn, and a prickly sensation came over him. "She never fails to go past the corral behind the barn first to check on the buckskin before doing her chores." He wanted to believe that it was KayCee's stab at matchmaking that accounted for her absence, but that inner voice he'd told Jenna about was telling him something else, something he didn't want to hear.

Jenna sensed his discomfort. "Trace? Is something wrong?"

"Hmm?" He forced his gaze back to hers. "It's nothing." But the uncomfortable feeling would not leave him. He glanced again in the direction of the corral. "I left the buckskin saddled up. I should go check on him."

Jenna cocked her head to one side and listened. "He sounds pretty quiet to me."

"A little too quiet."

"Maybe he's had time to think it over," she said. "Maybe you've won."

"That'll be the day. I have made some progress with him, though. Come on, want to see?" The air was clean and invigorating with the faint scent of autumn as they walked side by side toward the corral.

Trace didn't kid himself into thinking that Jenna had stayed for the love he had to offer. Nevertheless, he was touched by her love for KayCee.

"I don't suppose you're going to tell me what you two talked about," he ventured.

The look she gave him told him she'd die before she betrayed KayCee's confidence.

That was all right with him, though. Jenna had stayed, and that was all that mattered.

Chapter 14

The buckskin mustang stood in the middle of the corral, where Trace had left him. KayCee was sitting in the saddle, her legs not reaching the stirrups, the reins grasped in her ungloved hands.

"Trace, I had no idea this was the surprise!"

Jenna's startled voice reminded Trace that what he was seeing was real, when everything else told him it couldn't be, that he had to be dreaming.

"Neither did I."

His tone, frosty and taut, made her turn her head to look at him. "Oh, my God," she breathed when she saw that his face had gone all wooden and white. "You didn't know about this?"

The color that suddenly flooded his features, and the angry disbelief that brightened his black eyes, gave the answer. She could feel him gathering his strength about him and sensed the powerful reaction that was imminent. Her hand shot out to clamp over his forearm. His muscles were rigid and tense beneath her touch.

Half pleading, half demanding, she said, "Trace, please, don't ruin this for her."

His own voice emerged, tightly controlled through gritted teeth. "Jenna, if anyone ruins this for her, it'll be that horse. All I want to do is protect my kid."

Her grip tightened on his arm, fingers strengthening for emphasis. "Aren't you the one who said she has to learn on her own?"

His gaze left the two figures in the corral to burn into hers as if she'd gone insane. "Are you crazy? This is different. That horse can kill her."

"He's had his chance to do that, and he didn't," she argued. "Why don't you give him the benefit of the doubt? And while you're at it, why not have a little faith in KayCee? She has a way with that animal, Trace. Can't you see it?"

His gaze slid like ice back to the horse and rider, who, for the moment, were unaware that they were being watched. "He's too unpredictable."

"So are you," she countered.

"He's dangerous."

"So are you."

"Damn it, Jenna," he said in an angry whisper, "I would never hurt KayCee, but he might, even if only by accident."

"From what I saw when I first arrived a few months ago, you *were* hurting her, Trace, only you didn't know it. Now you do. What makes you think he can't learn the same lesson?''

"He's a horse, for Christ's sake. See the long tail, the mane, the hooves?''

"Yes, I see them." Then, in answer to his mocking tone, she smoothly added, "I also see another part of the horse standing before me right now. Care to guess which part?" She took that flare in his eyes for his reply. "Actually, you and he are a lot alike. You're both determined not to let the other one win."

"You make it sound like some kind of competition."

She shrugged with feigned indifference. "You said it, Trace. I didn't."

"Come on," he groaned. "That's ridiculous."

"Is it? Then why are you trying to force him to be something he's not? Could you be something you're not? Could you be anything other than Sioux?"

She hadn't asked him if he could be anything other than a man or a human being. Instead, she'd gone straight for the heart of his Indian soul, knowing that he was first and always Sioux. That was how well she knew him.

His dark eyes focused menacingly on her. "Of course not."

"Can KayCee be anything other than what she is, your daughter through and through? Isn't she proving that right now?"

She had a way of confounding him, of turning the tables and bringing the issue back around to what really mattered. "Are you suggesting that I should just let her sit there on him like that? And then what? Let her ride him? Give him to her?''

''It doesn't appear to be doing any harm at the moment,'' she observed. ''And isn't that really what life is all about? The moment?''

He didn't like the sound of his own words coming back at him, but neither could he dispute it. Despite his lenient method of rearing his daughter, his primary instinct was, first and foremost, to protect her. To stand by and do nothing went against the grain of every instinct he possessed.

''He looks perfectly calm to me,'' said Jenna.

''Yeah, well, looks can be deceiving.''

He knew that from the come-on look in her green eyes that competed with that crazy notion she had of forever. He'd been taught that only the earth and the sky lasted forever, but Jenna's belief that love, too, could last forever gave rise to uncertainty.

As a father, he'd have been perfectly within his rights to haul KayCee off that horse and send her straight to her room for having committed a terrible breach of his trust. But then he remembered what it was like to be twelve years old, and in the end it was the other side of him, the human side, that prevailed.

''All right, she can sit there a while longer. But if that horse makes one wrong move, he's history.''

''Why don't you duck out of sight for a few minutes, while I casually make my presence known? Then you can make your appearance and handle things as you see fit.''

Trace shook his head incredulously. "How could she think she could get away with this without me seeing her?"

"I guess she thought we'd be too involved with each other to notice. Or maybe she just figures some chances are worth taking."

He walked off, silently cursing his daughter's stubborn streak, which his permissiveness had had a hand in creating. He started for the house to get his rifle, but he didn't get very far before that sense of uncertainty began to peck at him again. His steps slowed to a halt. He thrust his hands into the pockets of his jeans and kicked at the dirt with his boot in angry frustration.

He didn't like waiting the requisite few minutes, but he was used to waiting. Hadn't he been waiting all his life for someone like Jenna to come along? Someone who could thrill him and dare him and leave him no place to hide?

Her ability to see past defenses might have put off another man, but for him there came a certain sense of freedom when there were no more dark corners in which to hide. He found it strangely quieting that she knew him as well as she did. Even now, as he paced back and forth, his bootheels wearing a path in the dirt, when he should have been furious at KayCee, he wasn't. The truth was, he was proud of his daughter, and he had Jenna to thank for it.

In the corral, KayCee was still mounted on Buck, a smile as big as Nebraska on her face.

"See? I knew he'd let me on him. I told you we were friends. I bet if I want him to, he'll even trot around the corral."

"KayCee, honey, maybe you should get down now," Jenna said gently from the other side of the fence. "There's no sense in trying to get him to do too much the first time you're on him. Maybe tomorrow your dad will let you—"

She didn't hear him come up behind her, but the air was suddenly filled with the charged tension of his presence. The smile dropped from KayCee's face, confirming what Jenna already knew.

"You were saying, Jenna?" he asked, his voice dangerously lazy, as he approached. He was looking right past her, to his daughter. "What might I let her do tomorrow?"

KayCee recognized that tone of voice and fell silent, knowing when not to argue. Although she demonstrated her disobedience with spiteful relish, she was still just a child, and the concern about being disciplined by her father outweighed any impulse to challenge him further.

"KayCee and I were just discussing how you were going to react to this," said Jenna. "She thinks you'll be angry. I agree. She also thinks you won't understand. That's where we disagree."

Why did she have to look at him like that, with those green eyes that always reminded him of the hills in springtime? Why was she forever challenging him? It infuriated him, yet it thrilled him all the same, for some part of him invariably rose to the challenge.

He turned abruptly to KayCee and called out to her, "Are you just going to sit there? See if you can get him going into a decent trot around the corral."

In answer to the relief he saw mirrored in Jenna's eyes, he said flippantly, "What the hell? If she's able to ride him, maybe it'll make it easier for me to train him."

But Jenna saw right through the practical reasoning to the softer impulse that prompted it. She felt a desperate tug on her heartstrings and turned her gaze toward the corral.

"Don't worry about the stirrups," Trace called to KayCee. "Pretend you're riding bareback. You've done that lots of times. Loosen up on the reins a little. Not too much. You don't want to give him the idea that he's in control. That's it. Be attentive, KayCee. Feel him beneath you. Try to anticipate his next move and give him a reason to do it your way."

KayCee appeared nervous in the saddle, but inasmuch as she'd been riding since she could walk, Jenna suspected that had more to do with wanting to please Trace than anything else.

"Go on," said Trace, "give him a tap."

KayCee put her heels to the buckskin's flanks and got no response.

"No, KayCee, not like you're asking him. Do it like you're telling him. And don't let up so much on the reins."

She gave the mustang a more forceful kick.

At first the horse did nothing. Then it gave a snort, a whinny and an impatient paw at the earth.

"Don't give him so much rein, KayCee! Go easy on the—"

Without warning, the buckskin sprinted forward and raced toward the far end of the corral. With KayCee holding on for dear life, he sailed into the air and over the fence.

A savage oath tore from Trace's lips.

Jenna forced her stricken gaze away from the horse that was galloping off toward the prairie to see Trace pivot sharply on his bootheels and dart off toward the house. With sickening certainty, she knew what he was doing.

She got to the house in time to see the screen door burst open from the force of his angry palm. It slammed loudly against its frame as he stormed outside, his rifle clutched in a deadly grip.

"Trace!"

She ran to him, but all the understanding had fled from his eyes, and she knew he was unapproachable. He was governed now by a more primal instinct, that of a parent to protect his young, and nothing she could do or say would change that.

With the easy lope of a wolf, he disappeared around the corner of the house and headed for the field where Teddy was grazing. Guessing his intention, Jenna darted off in the opposite direction, toward the barn.

She found the bay mare in the last stall and quickly bridled her. It had been years since she'd ridden without a saddle, but there wasn't time to waste. Positioning the mare beside a bale of hay, she climbed atop it and onto the bare back. With the hem of her long, loose skirt hiked above her knees to accommodate the horse's girth, she took off at a gallop after them.

She caught up with Trace in the foothills. He had dismounted and was kneeling with one knee on the ground, studying a patch of grass tamped down by passing hooves. She saw him pick something up and put it in the pocket of his cowhide vest. Then he rose to his six-foot height, grasped a fistful of coarse mane and jumped onto the bare red back as if he had sprouted wings.

Without the aid of a bridle, he guided Teddy over to where Jenna was waiting and cast a quick glance at her long, bare legs. Something stirred inside him when he recalled what it felt like to have those silky legs wrapped around him. He pulled his gaze away.

"They're headed in this direction."

With a subtle tensing of his knees, he turned the sorrel's head away. She followed at an easy canter, grateful for the denim jacket that warded off the chill that swept down from the hills and over the plains.

The aspens were vibrant with autumn color. The streams they splashed through were knife-bright and icy-cold. The moon, nearly full, was visible in the clear blue sky. In a couple of hours the sun would be down, and it was not uncommon for the temperature in the foothills to drop to around freezing at night. With the coming of darkness, it would be difficult even for someone with Trace's tracking experience to follow the buckskin's path.

There was no time for arguments between them, no recriminations or reproaches. They had to find KayCee before dark.

They rode on into the afternoon at a tireless pace, while overhead the sky slowly turned from the clear, bright cerulean of day to the deep, crystalline blue of dusk.

Trace knew his way over the wild land as he knew how to breathe. This was the land of his forefathers. It was his life, his soul, and yet it meant nothing without his daughter, for she was his heart, and if that ceased to beat, all else would cease, also. Like a wolf stalking prey, determined and utterly relentless, he rode with a singular purpose, to find her, following a route known only to him.

Jenna wanted to believe that he knew where he was going, but his stoic silence was driving her crazy and she was growing increasingly worried.

"Trace, it's getting darker. What if—"

"Shh!"

His attempt to silence her only made matters worse.

"How can you you sit there like that without saying a word?" she said, exasperation finally getting the best of her.

Trace expelled an impatient breath into the chill air. "Jenna, you're going to have to learn to be still and to listen."

"Listen to what?" she exclaimed. "You don't really expect to hear a voice rise from the distance, shouting, 'Hey, she's over here,' do you?"

"Hardly. But aside from the sound of our horses' hooves, tell me what you hear."

"Nothing," she said indignantly.

"That's right. Nothing. No sounds. No birds in the trees, no crickets in the grass, no deer moving through the brush. There's a silence in the air that says someone has recently passed this way. If you'd be quiet, you could hear it, too. Be attentive," he told her.

The shadows of twilight danced in Jenna's green eyes when she looked at him inquisitively. "You said the same thing to KayCee earlier."

"It's a simple message, really. Among my people it means that in every act, in every thing, at every instant, there's the presence of something greater than yourself. You can call it God, or Allah, or just the way things are. To the Sioux it's the Great Spirit, and one must be always and intensely attentive to his presence. He is within everything—the trees, the rivers, the mountains, even that mean-tempered mustang. And only by being attentive to his presence can we understand the things around us, including the silence."

She knew now why he was able to pick out signs of the mustang's passing when none was visible to the naked eye. It came not only from an acquired skill for tracking, but also from a much deeper part of him. It was something she might never truly understand, yet she loved him all the more for it, because it made him unlike any man she'd ever known.

Trusting Trace's Indian instincts quelled Jenna's apprehension, and silence came easier to her after that. With a stillness that came from within, she began to notice the things around her, like the great streaks of purple that stretched across the eastern sky, and she began to feel awed by it.

Trace rode at an easy canter beside her, his body moving in rhythm to the sorrel's gait, now and again stealing peeks at her. It was hard to believe that at a time like this he could notice anything except a constricting sense of panic at the need to locate KayCee before nightfall, but the sight of Jenna's face bathed in the golden light of dusk as she gazed eastward was impossible for him to ignore.

He was glad she'd had the temerity to come along. The thought of his daughter alone in the wild country at night sent unparalleled fear racing through him, and despite his having been abrupt with Jenna for talking too much, it was only the sound of her husky voice that kept him firmly anchored.

"I'm glad you're here," he said.

Jenna's head spun around. "So am I. I just hope—" She bit her lip at the hasty words that nearly slipped out before she could stop them.

"We'll find her," he said.

No *ifs*, no *whens*, only an arrogant confidence she found hard to share.

"What makes you so sure?" she asked.

"Because I know where he's taking her."

He nodded toward the hills up ahead, which were studded with pines. "I caught him in a meadow just beyond those hills this spring and herded him in with the others. That's where he's headed."

"Is KayCee with him?"

"She was the last time I spotted his tracks, and that was a couple of miles back."

"How do you know that?"

"Because the tracks were deeper than he makes on his own. He was still carrying a rider."

Jenna's heart began to beat faster. "What are we waiting for? Come on, let's go!"

He reached over and grabbed hold of the reins before she could turn the mare's head in the direction of the hills.

"If we ride in there like our tails are on fire, we'll only scare him away. That meadow is his home, and we're going to ride in nice and easy from where he least expects it, the back door."

Such icy determination was in sharp contrast to the hot-blooded, undisciplined side of his nature, yet Jenna found it no less compelling. "And then what?" she dared to ask.

He answered honestly, "I don't know." But as he turned his horse's head in the direction of the hills, his fingers tightened around the rifle he still clutched in his hand.

Chapter 15

They moved at an easy, unseen pace through the cover of the trees until they came to the opposite side of the meadow and found themselves facing east.

The sky was the deep purple of early evening. Ringed by fiery hillsides, the meadow looked like a stage, illuminated by the golden light of the setting sun. In its center, about a hundred yards away, was a ribbon of water. Beside it, the silhouette of the buckskin stallion was etched against the panorama.

Trace's heart skipped a beat and his body flooded with relief when he saw KayCee rise up from the ground, where she had been on her belly, drinking water from the stream.

The supercharged silence was broken by the sound of his whisper. "Wait here."

"What are you going to do?" Jenna whispered back.

"I'm going to get my daughter."

"You can't just ride over there. He'll take one look at you and run for the hills."

"Do you have a better idea?"

"Yes."

She threw her leg over the mare's shoulders and jumped to the ground.

In less than a heartbeat, Trace dismounted and blocked her path. In a furious whisper, he demanded, "What do you think you're doing?"

"There's no other way," said Jenna. "He has no reason to hate me, so maybe he won't run away."

"You just don't get it, do you? That's a dangerous animal. He could hurt KayCee."

Jenna looked at the buckskin, who stood with one rear hoof leisurely bent, his head down, soft, fleshy lips nibbling on meadow grass.

"No, Trace," she said, turning to look into his handsome and angry face, "I think you're the one who doesn't get it. If he wanted to hurt her, he'd have done it. Stop being so pigheaded. Be attentive!"

Ebony eyes locked in silent combat with her bold green ones, which refused to look away. It took courage for her to use those words on him. At one time, he might have bitterly questioned what she knew about being Indian or if she understood what it was like for him to have a heart that beat in rhythm with everything else around him. But he had long ago ceased questioning her capacity for understanding.

Jenna need not be from his world to understand him. It seemed to come naturally to her, as if she were meant for him and him alone. It wasn't just the way her slender body fit so perfectly with his. It was the courage that brightened her eyes, the spirit with which she tested him. She was proof that it was not always necessary to experience that which the heart knew to be true.

This white woman with the sparkling green eyes and feisty nature understood him better than he understood himself at times. Like now, telling him to be attentive. Bless her bold little heart, she knew exactly what she was doing.

Trace swallowed hard and said, "This is my battle, Jenna. I started it. I'll finish it. Like I said, you wait here."

The look in his black eyes was unreadable, but she could tell by the plaintive sound of his whisper, devoid now of any harshness, that something was different.

"Hold this for me, would you?"

Her gaze dropped wordlessly to the rifle. There was no sign of reluctance in the strong brown hand that held it out to her. She took it and stepped aside for him to move past her.

"Trace?"

The sound of his name, carried on her husky whisper, turned him around. His black hair fell unrestricted to his shoulders. The lean angles of his face were softened to near perfection when caught in the dispersed light of the setting sun. His eyes, those beautiful obsidian orbs from which his emotions spilled, looked at her expectantly.

"Good luck," she whispered.

He patted the pocket of his vest and, smiling slyly to himself, as if with some secret meaning, said, "That's already been assured." Like the wind moving noiselessly over the prairie, he walked off, rustling not a single fallen leaf on the ground beneath his feet.

A chill careened down Jenna's spine. She turned up the collar of Trace's denim jacket and jammed her hands down into the pockets for warmth, but her actions had nothing to do with the temperature. Rather, it was his lean and lithe body moving away from her, the animallike strides carrying him deeper into the evening shadows, the scent of him that lingered in the air, that chilled her to the marrow.

As she waited among the trees for Trace to return, Jenna became aware of the rustlings in the undergrowth of some small creature awakening for an evening forage. She felt the caress of the wind upon her face and smelled the faint fragrance of Trace carried back to her on currents of air. But most of all, she heard the sound of her own inner voice, telling her to be still, to listen, to be attentive to everything around her and everything within. And in those few minutes everything seemed to change, to meld and to mesh in a way she had never experienced before. It was as if there were indeed no beginning and no ending, as if all that mattered were the moment, and the moment was Trace.

She watched his tall, lean figure moving across the darkening distance toward his daughter. They were both right, father and daughter, and too much alike for there to ever be any real peace between them. KayCee would be forever testing Trace, and he would forever resist it. Could it be that they needed the balance of a third party in their lives—a wife and mother, for instance?

Jenna bit down hard on her lip to stifle the moan that welled up inside her, caused by the desperate desire she had to be that third party in their lives.

Jenna saw the stallion lift its head at Trace's approach and retreat to a safe distance, while Trace spoke quietly with KayCee for several minutes before leading her away.

When they reached her, she put her foolish notions aside and asked eagerly, "What happened?"

Not even the growing darkness could conceal the look of utter sadness on KayCee's face. Tears glistened in her eyes as she turned her face up to Jenna.

"I'm sorry, Jenna. I didn't mean to worry you and Dad like that. I didn't think about what might happen. I just wanted to show you how good Buck can be. I love Buck. He's the only friend I've got. He's the only one who understands."

Jenna was touched by her pathos. "I'm your friend."

KayCee's gaze dropped shyly to the ground. "I was hoping you'd be more than that. I was hoping you'd be my mom. But I guess you don't love my dad."

"That's not true," Jenna exclaimed. "I do love your father. I love him very much."

"Then how come you're not together?"

"But we are together. We both came to find you, didn't we?"

"That's not what I mean."

"Sometimes we have no control over who we love," said Jenna. "Right or wrong, it just happens. But what's even more important is that your father loves you."

"But when you love someone," said KayCee, "don't you want to give them the thing they want the most?"

Like giving Trace the moment, Jenna thought with a groan. Oh, God, he was right. It was her own rigid notion of what love should be that stood between them. She swallowed down the painful knot in her throat and said hesitantly, "Well, yes."

"And if my dad loved me, he'd give me the thing I want the most, wouldn't he?"

Trace was stunned by Jenna's confession, partly because that was exactly the way it was for him, uncontrollable and inevitable, but mostly because with it came the realization that this was no longer a crazy dream. This was the real thing.

There was no sign of annoyance in his voice, only that matter-of-fact tone he sometimes used that made KayCee bristle. "You'd be a fool to judge how much I love you by what I give you. But assuming there is something I can give you that would prove how much I love you, before I ask what it is, tell me why you disobeyed me."

KayCee shrugged in an exaggerated, childish gesture. "You told me once that a friend's the best thing you can have, and Buck's my friend."

He vaguely recalled saying something to that effect in one of the many speeches he'd given her over the years. "Weren't you scared?"

"Not of Buck," she replied.

It was so simple to her, this issue that seemed so complex and insurmountable to him. He looked at Jenna and saw her eyes burning bright with encouragement and expectation.

"Oh, what the hell?" he said. "I can't fight you both. All right, KayCee, you have my word that I won't sell Buck to anyone. We'll keep him. Besides, Teddy's getting old, and Buck shows signs of one day being a decent cutter."

Jenna rushed forward on impulse and placed a kiss upon his cheek. "Oh, Trace, I knew you'd do it!" she cried with a joyous laugh.

"Try to control yourself, Jenna. I didn't exactly part the Red Sea. And in case you haven't noticed, the recipient of my generosity doesn't seem to share your enthusiasm."

Standing off to the side, KayCee did not look like a little girl whose wish had just come true.

Trace shook his head and said, "You two wait for me here. This shouldn't take long."

He made his way back to where Teddy was grazing, grasped a fistful of coarse mane and jumped onto the sorrel's bare back. In moments he was galloping hard toward the buckskin, the lasso whirling over his head.

The buckskin took off, clods of dark earth flying from its hooves, and disappeared into the woods on the opposite side of the meadow with Trace, astride Teddy, in hot pursuit.

The chase took them through woods and valleys and splashing through streams. The mustang was a clever creature and managed to evade the rope. It ran as if its tail were on fire, faster than Trace had ever seen him run.

The chase ended in a canyon. With only one way in and one way out, the stallion was trapped. He stood against the far canyon wall, pawing the earth, the look in his eyes seeming to acknowledge that the battle was over.

The rope sailed into the air and landed around the buckskin's neck.

Yet as he led the mustang out of the canyon, Trace felt no triumph, only a weariness that came not from his muscles but from a place deep inside him. He was tired of fighting, not just the horse, but himself, too. He had always assumed that breaking the buckskin was all that mattered, but Jenna had proved him wrong. She'd had the courage to see the truth and speak out against his pigheadedness. And so had KayCee, only twelve years old and yet wiser than him in so many ways.

He was proud of his daughter for accomplishing something he'd been unable to do, all because she treated the horse like a friend, and because she trusted and understood him in ways Trace did not. He thought himself the fool, for reminding KayCee to be attentive when he was the one who needed the reminding. And for telling Jenna that it was the moment that counted when, unlike him, she was unwilling to settle for anything less than forever. He loved them both, as fiercely as it was possible for a man to love. And to think he'd almost lost them.

Trace brought Teddy to a halt. Behind him, the buckskin waited nervously, at the end of the rope. For Trace, the moment of truth had arrived. He dismounted and walked to the buckskin.

There was no warning snort from flared nostrils, no sharp hoof pawing the earth, only a soft nicker that seemed to acknowledge a grudging respect. He let the man come near and stood perfectly still as the hands he knew so well moved quickly yet gently over him to remove the heavy tooled saddle and woolen saddle blanket from his back. Then the man moved to the horse's head and looked deeply into his eyes for many long moments before removing the bridle from its face and the iron bit from its mouth.

What Trace did next didn't frighten the mustang so much as startle him. He reached out and clamped strong fingers over its fleshy muzzle and brought it close to his face. He inhaled deeply several times, drawing the horse's breath into his human lungs. Then he forced several of his own hot breaths into the horse's nostrils, which this time did flare wide.

It took no more than seconds to accomplish, and then it was over.

"Now I have your spirit within me," Trace whispered to the stallion. "And mine will be always within you."

He ran his open palm across the bristly coat of the buckskin's neck, partly in a gesture of grudging friendship, partly as if to say, "See, I can touch you now, and you'll let me."

In the end, they both won. For Trace, the triumph came in letting go. For the buckskin mustang, it came with a solid slap on the rump that sent it galloping off to freedom.

Trace watched as the mustang faded into the shadows that had gathered over the open meadow, then mounted and turned Teddy's head toward the two who were waiting for him.

KayCee knew her father was too good at what he did not to have captured the buckskin. When she saw him return alone, she knew what had happened. She flew into his arms and smothered his face with wet kisses. "Oh, thank you, Dad! Thank you!" she cried.

"Now do you know how much I love you?"

Her face was split in a grin from ear to ear. "You bet!"

"Good. Then why don't you show me how much you love me and jump on that mare and go wait for me over by those trees?"

"What are you gonna do?" she asked.

"Something I should have done a long time ago."

He took her by the hand and led her over to the bay mare. Cupping his hands he received her foot and lifted her effortlessly onto the horse's back.

Jenna was standing beside Teddy when he returned. She looked at him—almost shyly, it seemed—

and said, "I'm proud of you, Trace. It took courage to do what you did."

"No, it didn't. It took love."

"You certainly have KayCee's love. But she would love you even if you didn't let Buck go."

"I'm not talking about how much KayCee loves me."

"Oh. You mean what I said before? It's true. I can't deny that I've fallen in love with you."

"I wasn't talking about that, either. Jenna, there's something I have to say."

"That's all right, Trace. You don't have to explain."

"Explain what?"

"That you don't love me. At least not in the way that I love you."

"But that's what I'm trying to tell you."

She looked at him questioningly, not daring to hope, yet unable to stop herself.

His voice dropped low, the way it did whenever it was filled with emotion. "I do love you, Jenna. More than I ever thought it was possible to love a woman."

With those few simple words, he felt something give inside him, like the wall of a dam bursting from the pressure of the rushing water within. With it went the doubt, the bitterness, the prejudice, the mustang, and everything else that didn't matter. Suddenly it was so easy to say *I love you* to the woman who had helped set his own heart free.

"I couldn't have let Buck go if it weren't for you, no matter how much it meant to KayCee. Without you I could never have understood what KayCee was going through, or what's been missing in my life. You, Jenna. You're what's missing.''

He took her hands in his and drew her to him. In a soft voice, he murmured, ''Do you remember those blizzards I told you about? Well, sometimes it snows so hard you can't leave the house for days. When I know a blizzard's coming I send KayCee up to my mother's. If you were to, say, just for argument's sake, marry me, you'd have to spend a lot of time indoors with me. There wouldn't be anybody but us for, who knows, maybe weeks at a time? Do you think you can stand that?''

Jenna's heart raced with joy. ''Trace McCall, if that's a marriage proposal, it's the strangest one I've ever heard.''

He pulled her closer with instinctive possessiveness. ''And how many of them have you heard?''

''Only one that matters.''

''And your answer?''

''Yes, I'll marry you. I'll be yours.''

With a touch as light as air, he brushed a strand of chestnut hair from her face with the tip of his finger, while the fingers of his other hand burned with exquisite pain into her flesh, pulling her closer, until her lips met his.

''Mitawin,'' he breathed. ''My woman. I love you. Love you.''

He bent his head to kiss her, to seal with his lips that which he had claimed as his own from the start.

Just as he had exchanged spirits with the mustang, Trace felt Jenna's spirit invading his through the warm, moist breath that mingled with his own.

Jenna's joy was complete. In those dark eyes that had once been shadowed by so much distrust, she saw only blinding love. In his gentle Sioux words, she heard forever.

He placed his hands around her waist and lifted her into the air and onto Teddy's bare back. The hard-muscled wall of his chest came up against her back when he jumped up behind her. The press of his legs against hers and his arms going around her to grasp the coarse mane sent waves of undisciplined pleasure through her. She could tell by the biting press of his anatomy against her how much it was affecting him, as well.

She leaned pliantly against him, feeling warmed by the heat of his body, protected by the strength of his arms, but most of all loved by the power of his spirit.

In a warm rush of breath at her ear, he said, "Earlier today I found this."

He reached into the pocket of his cowhide vest and took out a spear of grama grass bearing four heads. He twirled it between his thumb and forefinger before her eyes.

"It brings good luck in love," he said.

They met KayCee at the edge of the meadow, and together they ascended the gently sloping land into the foothills. At the top of a rise, they paused. The amethyst sky was streaked with clouds tinted saffron by the glow of the setting sun. Beyond them the prairie stretched for as far as the eye could see, blending into the shadows of approaching night and disappearing from view. The autumn wind passed over the grass, rustling the tall blades, creating a momentum that had no beginning and no ending, starting with a moment and lasting forever.

* * * * *

COMING NEXT MONTH

MILLION DOLLAR SWEEPSTAKES (III)

No purchase necessary. To enter the sweepstakes and receive the Free Books and Surprise Gift, follow the directions published and complete and mail your "Win A Fortune" Game Card. If not taking advantage of the book and gift offer or if the "Win A Fortune" Game Card is missing, you may enter by hand-printing your name and address on a 3" X 5" card and mailing it (limit: one entry per envelope) via First Class Mail to: Million Dollar Sweepstakes (III) "Win A Fortune" Game, P.O. Box 1867, Buffalo, NY 14269-1867, or Million Dollar Sweepstakes (III) "Win A Fortune" Game, P.O. Box 609, Fort Erie, Ontario L2A 5X3. When your entry is received, you will be assigned sweepstakes numbers. To be eligible entries must be received no later than March 31, 1996. No liability is assumed for printing errors or lost, late or misdirected entries. Odds of winning are determined by the number of eligible entries distributed and received.

Sweepstakes open to residents of the U.S. (except Puerto Rico), Canada, Europe and Taiwan who are 18 years of age or older. All applicable laws and regulations apply. Sweepstakes offer void wherever prohibited by law. Values of all prizes are in U.S. currency. This sweepstakes is presented by Torstar Corp, its subsidiaries and affiliates, in conjunction with book, merchandise and/or product offerings. For a copy of the official rules governing this sweepstakes offer, send a self-addressed, stamped envelope (WA residents need not affix return postage) to: MILLION DOLLAR SWEEPSTAKES (III) Rules, P.O. Box 4573, Blair, NE 68009, USA.

SWP-S1295

Are your lips succulent, impetuous, delicious or racy?

Find out in a very special Valentine's Day promotion—THAT SPECIAL KISS!

Inside four special Harlequin and Silhouette February books are details for THAT SPECIAL KISS! explaining how you can have your lip prints read by a romance expert.

Look for details in the following series books, written by four of Harlequin and Silhouette readers' favorite authors:

Silhouette Intimate Moments #691
Mackenzie's Pleasure by *New York Times* bestselling author Linda Howard

Harlequin Romance #3395
Because of the Baby by Debbie Macomber

Silhouette Desire #979
Megan's Marriage by Annette Broadrick

Harlequin Presents #1793
The One and Only by Carole Mortimer

Fun, romance, four top-selling authors, plus a FREE gift! This is a very special Valentine's Day you won't want to miss! Only from Harlequin and Silhouette.

VAL96

INTRODUCING...

A collection of award-winning books by award-winning authors! From Harlequin and Silhouette.

Falling Angel
by Anne Stuart

WINNER OF THE RITA AWARD FOR BEST ROMANCE!

Falling Angel by Anne Stuart is a RITA Award winner, voted Best Romance. A truly wonderful story, *Falling Angel* will transport you into a world of hidden identities, second chances and the magic of falling in love.

"Ms. Stuart's talent shines like the brightest of stars, making it very obvious that her ultimate destiny is to be the next romance author at the top of the best-seller charts."
—*Affaire de Coeur*

A heartwarming story for the holidays. You won't want to miss award-winning *Falling Angel*, available this January wherever Harlequin and Silhouette books are sold.

Silhouette

SPECIAL EDITION ™ ®

CELEBRATION 1000

It's our 1000th Special Edition and we're celebrating!

Join us these coming months for some wonderful stories in a special celebration of our 1000th book with some of your favorite authors!

Diana Palmer　　　**Nora Roberts**
Debbie Macomber　　**Christine Flynn**
Phyllis Halldorson　　**Lisa Jackson**

Plus miniseries by:

Lindsay McKenna, Marie Ferrarella, Sherryl Woods and Gina Ferris Wilkins.

And many more books by special writers!

And as a special bonus, all Silhouette Special Edition titles published during Celebration 1000! will have **<u>double</u>** Pages & Privileges proofs of purchase!

Silhouette Special Edition...heartwarming stories packed with emotion, just for you! You'll fall in love with our next 1000 special stories!

You're About to Become a *Privileged* *Woman*

Reap the rewards of fabulous free gifts and benefits with proofs-of-purchase from Silhouette and Harlequin books

Pages & Privileges™

It's our way of thanking you for buying our books at your favorite retail stores.

PROOF OF PURCHASE
SIM-PP86
Offer expires October 31, 1996

Pages & Privileges ™

Harlequin and Silhouette— the most privileged readers in the world!

For more information about Harlequin and Silhouette's PAGES & PRIVILEGES program call the Pages & Privileges Benefits Desk: 1-503-794-2499

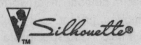

Silhouette®

SIM-PP86